I0685744

BATTLE EARTH XI

NICK S. THOMAS

BATTLE EARTH XI

NICK S. THOMAS

PROLOGUE

From Colonel Mitch Taylor's personal journal - Uncharted space, Day 62

We came out here to run and hide. That almost failed, and then the most surprising of encounters. Once again I find myself facing an alien race I had never heard of or known of their existence. At first they attacked, as we have come to expect from aliens, but now there is silence. We fought a common enemy when we were forced to do so. They let us leave their planet without bloodshed, but will they join us?

It's been a month since we drove the Krys forces out of the system, and still we wait. Not allowed to set foot on the planet, unable to move on without risk of defeat at the hands of Erdogan's fleet. We cannot see them. We do not know where they are, but the threat looms over us all the time. Everyone knows our fate lies with the decision of an alien race we cannot even come close to knowing or understanding. Nobody says it, but everything thinks it. How can we trust this alien race? How can we trust them to be any better? But what is the alternative?

CHAPTER ONE

Kelly sat at a desk, looking at data that both bored and worried him, food, water, and ammunition. The Drachenburg was well stocked, but they had been expending the resources at a great rate. There were no easy answers to the problems they faced. He rubbed his brow and tried to think of how they could access more resources. He wore a full Reitech suit, and his rifle lay on the desk beside him. He was sure to be ready to fight at any time he was awake.

"Not easy, is it, Sir?" Lieutenant Engel asked.

He shook his head. Resources in against resources out, easy enough to calculate what we need, just not how to get it," he replied, "Any ideas?"

"The land continues to provide much of what we need in food and water, but ammunition will not be easy. We must soon venture out far further afield. Military bases, storage depots, we will have to reach them."

"Most of them will have been flattened, or watched at the very least."

She did not reply.

"I don't suppose we have a choice, do we?"

Engel shook her head.

They could hear a flurry of activity outside, and Kelly could tell he needed to get out there and deal with it. He jumped out of his chair, snatched up his rifle, and headed for the entrance to the open air where they had first arrived and met Becker. They saw two vehicles coming into view, and one was already parked outside with several personnel rushing to assist the crew. Even through the crowd, he could see the familiar scorch marks on the vehicle that were caused by Krys pulse weapons. Screams rang out from the wounded.

Shit, this doesn't look good, he thought.

Two crew were hauled from the vehicle. A woman, whose face and shoulder were burnt and her armour heavily damaged. The other a man; his left arm was missing, and he had shrapnel embedded in the flank of his armour beneath the limbless joint. One of the other vehicles slid to a halt beside them, and Becker leapt out. His own truck had also been hit, with half the roll cage gone as well as the tailgate.

"What happened?" Kelly demanded.

"They were waiting for us. Reeled us in until we were

right where they wanted us. We didn't stand a chance."

"You fell into their trap?" Kelly asked sceptically, "Did you get away clean?"

Becker shook his head. "I don't know."

"What do you mean, you don't know? You don't know? Captain, the secret location of this facility is the number one most important thing in our lives!"

"I said I don't know, okay!" he yelled back.

Kelly looked around to see that no one else was coming up to join them. There was a vehicle missing and several personnel.

"Casualties?" he asked in a calmer voice.

Becker nodded.

"Fredrickson, he didn't even see it coming. Vehicle was a fireball before we even knew they were hitting us."

"But did you get away clean?" demanded Kelly once again.

Becker ignored the question and continued around his vehicle, helping out his driver who was also wounded. Kelly could tell the Captain really did have no idea. He shook his head. He already knew the answer wouldn't be good. He turned back to the entrance to the bunker, where several of his people stood awaiting some response, while others continued to give medical aid and haul the wounded inside.

Kelly opened his mouth to speak, but he could not think of anything to say. He turned away and thought for a moment. Before anything came into his head, he noticed a red flash of light come from behind him and turned to see the silent warning beacon light flash beside the bunker.

"They're here," he said to them.

Many of them looked worried. Even a few attending the wounded stopped and looked to him for answers. Before he could say a word, one of his own people point the finger at Becker.

"You led them here. You've killed us all!"

"We were out there fighting and dying today for all of us!" Becker shouted back.

"We should have gone ourselves; piss poor excuse for soldiers this lot!"

Kelly leapt forward and stood between them as the two men rushed at each other, ready to start an all out war among themselves.

"Pack it in!" he ordered.

They backed off and all went silent, waiting for him to continue.

"Whatever is coming for us, we aren't done yet! I told you the only thing we exist to do now is kill as many of those bastards as we could in the time we had left. So they're coming for us. Targets for our guns, a chance to up our kill count. You all know what to do. Take up positions!"

Nobody moved for a few seconds, and then suddenly they leapt into motion as if responding with muscle memory.

"Lock this place down!"

Becker was rushing past him, but Kelly reached out and stopped him.

"Finally time to put that armour to use."

Becker nodded in agreement.

"Not exactly what I had in mind, but we'll do our duty."

He reached for the foliage covering his tank, dragging it away to reveal the vehicle all ready to move as the rest of his crew climbed aboard. He leapt onto the hull and looked back to Kelly one last time.

"You know this is the end, right?"

"Yeah, maybe. But, Captain, I've heard that so many times, it is starting to get a little boring. Maybe I don't believe it anymore. Maybe we really are immortal."

"Like Colonel Taylor and his hooligans…the Immortals? Maybe that nickname was given a little hastily."

"Yes, and maybe they are still alive up there, somewhere. If I know Taylor, he's probably kicking back and enjoying himself right about now. Taking in a new life somewhere far from all this."

"And you really believe that?"

"I like to think so. If only because it makes me laugh to think of him living in defiance of these bastards."

"Isn't that what we're doing?"

"Yes. Let's focus on that living part. We might get out of this yet."

Becker laughed as he climbed into the top turret and pulled his helmet on. Kelly left to go about his business. Even over the sound of the tanks firing up, he could hear the roar of Mech engines in the sky and explosions half a kilometre away at their outer perimeter.

Kelly wanted to go forward with them to the front, but he knew he had to stay put. Everyone knew their part, and they were promptly falling into place. Becker rocked as his driver rolled the vehicle forwards and quickly accelerated to the northern entrance. The thick forest and rocks kept the bunker well hidden and funnelled the armour down a few narrow corridors. But Kelly was certain it would not be long before airborne infantry hit them.

As he stepped back into the bunker, he headed for the anti-aircraft control room. He stepped in and found a man and a woman sitting at the controls. They were little more than screens and joysticks; the guns on the roof were remotely controlled from deep within the reinforced roof of the facility.

"Ready?" he asked them.

He didn't know either of their names, but it didn't matter anymore.

"You used these systems before?"

"Not in anger," replied the woman.

"You will soon enough."

* * *

Becker could hear the fire loud and clear now, and as he ducked down inside the turret, a pulse raced just a few metres overhead. He quickly hit the hatch switch so that it slid across above him, and finally he was encased in the turret's armour. It was comforting to be within the vehicle, but he also remembered all to well how fearsome the Mech weapons could be.

Two of the vehicles in his squadron were already positioned ahead in hull down positions they had dug out weeks before.

"All right, boys," he said through the comms system, "Weeks of pissing about in soft skin rubbish, time to bring out the big guns. Let's show them what we've got."

His driver brought them right up to the defence lines without him having to say a word. They all knew the plan well enough. Before they had come to a halt, a Mech vehicle came into view, and Becker looked on his display screens. The gunner had already taken aim with their stabilised gun.

"Fire!" he shouted.

The shot rang out just as they came to a standstill, and Becker watched with glee. The powerful round struck the lower hull of the enemy vehicle and went through it with little resistance at all. Even though he could see it was one of their lighter assault vehicles, it still brought a smile to his face.

The auto-loading magazine fed cannon was good to

go in less than two seconds after the impact, and Becker was already looking for targets. The commander's seat in the turret viewed a display screen a metre tall that showed their surroundings. It almost gave the impression he was all alone out in the wilderness. Up above him were four screens giving a view overhead. He looked up to see Mech aircraft passing overhead.

"Damn, that didn't take them long."

"Why don't they just bomb us to hell?" asked Cody, the driver.

"Maybe they fancied a fight, just as we did," replied Becker.

He knew it was an unlikely reason, but he couldn't find anything better to say. He caught a glimmer of movement on one screen and looked carefully at another Mech vehicle passing through the foliage up ahead. The armour-clad warriors at its flanks surrounded it.

"All right, you sons of bitches, let's take that mother down!"

His gunner quickly traversed the gun, and Becker yelled, "Fire!"

The shot glanced off the sloped frontal armour.

"Shit," Becker said to himself.

He opened his mouth to voice further commands, but the gunner was already ahead of him. He had taken aim low on the vehicle's hull. Becker nodded in approval.

"Fire!"

The shot rang out, and their target ignited into flames, causing the troops either side to scatter.

"Hell, yes! Must have hit something serious!"

Pulses flashed out from the vehicle in all directions as if the ammunition had gone off.

"Another few of those, please!" Becker called out.

He grinned to himself and studied the scene before them again, as Cody opened up with the two hull-mounted Reitech machine guns. They tore through the Mechs who still advanced on them, despite their losses. Becker reached across to his controls and hit the play button on his own personal choice of music. It was classic German metal, and he cranked it up loud. He nodded, taking in the atmosphere and shouting, "Fire!" as another enemy vehicle came into view. Just as before, they aimed low, and it burst into flames.

He could see more aircraft closing in on his screens overhead but knew he had to rely on others to deal with them. He looked back to his screens and smiled. Just as Becker was starting to enjoy himself, a huge flash burst on their right side. He was forced to look away from the screens to avoid being blinded.

As the light faded, he saw several of the side cameras of their vehicle had been destroyed, and all he could see were a few wisps of smoke at the edge of the front and rear cameras. Despite being unable to see the carnage for himself, he knew the vehicle beside them had been utterly destroyed by a devastating hit. He shook his head; he knew every one of the crew well. But he quickly turned his attention back to what was going on ahead.

The gunner, Christian, was aimed on target and awaiting the command to fire.

"What are you waiting for?" he demanded, "Fire, and keep firing!"

The turret immediately rocked as the gun sprang to life. Becker turned his attention to movement at the top of the screen in front of him. He could see a large and bulky aircraft dip and begin a strafing run towards them.

"Incoming!"

He knew they could do nothing against aerial targets but hope their armour was sufficient, and that their allies were covering them. Barrels on the wings flashed from pulse cannons firing, and the shots landed all around them. Tracer fire rushed towards the craft as the bunkers' weapons fired back, but they seemed to have little effect.

Becker saw flashes beneath his feet where a pulse ripped into the hull of the tank; he knew Cody could not have survived it. Another few pulses struck their tank, throwing shrapnel about the interior. One piece embedded in Becker's helmet, and the force of the impact snapped his head back into the padded cushion behind.

As he opened his eyes again, he could see the gunner's screen tilt up and Christian trying to take aim at the aircraft as it was closing in and coming right for them. It was an impossible shot, but as pulses punched holes in their vehicle, he knew they had just seconds left.

"Do it, Christian!"

Another pulse ripped through the hull and cut Christian's left leg off at the knee. He let out a scream in agony.

"Christian! Hit them! Fire!"

He squeezed the trigger. There was a flash, and the shot left the barrel, hitting the incoming aircraft just off centre of the nose. Becker could barely make out the shape of the wreck hurtling towards them and engulfed in flames. He had no time left to move and could do nothing but hope for the best.

"Fuck you!" he screamed at the screen. The aircraft crashed into his vehicle with an almighty smash that rocked the vehicle violently, and part of the craft embedded itself in the vehicle like a spear into a boar.

* * *

"That doesn't sound good," said Captain Reynolds.

Kelly nodded in agreement.

"The guns are still firing, is that a good thing?"

"Well it means we're still in the fight, and that we haven't won it. Take your pick of the good and bad news."

The anti-aircraft weapons above continued to roar as they had done for several minutes.

"We've got incoming Mechs!" a voice shouted.

"All right, here they come," said Kelly.

He stepped up to a bunker slit just two metres beside one of the gun emplacements. It only took a few seconds for him to spot the first few Mechs descend into the open ground where Becker had arrived with his convoy, and what now seemed like hours before.

"Led them right to us," said Reynolds.

"Doesn't matter anymore. We can't change it. All we can do is...fire!"

The heavy weapon rattled into action and sent heavy Reitech rounds hurtling towards the Mechs at eight hundred rounds per minute. None of their infantry weapons could manage anything like it, for either the limited box magazine capacities or heat build up on the barrels. The heavy weapon was shielded and had a broad coolant chamber surrounding the barrel. It resembled a weapon more akin to the early twentieth century, but that was where the similarities stopped.

Kelly took aim and fired two careful shots at one creature that had just landed and before it could get into motion. A pulse smashed into the wall next to him, and on impact sent drops of burning pulse matter over the slit. He saw some of it splash onto the handrail of his rifle and smoke gush from it. He took another shot, and then the fourth jammed.

"Shit," he muttered to himself.

He threw the rifle into the far side of the bunker and

picked up another lying strategically against the wall beside him with three others, as if he never intended to change a magazine at all, but rather go from one rifle to another. He began firing once again and could now see the hundreds of shots were knocking down the few dozen Mechs that had landed ahead of them. He stopped firing and watched the work of his people; the Mechs were cut down in a turkey shoot.

The shooting finally died down, and ecstatic cheers soon followed the silence from the defensive lines, running fifty metres in either direction. He looked out at the smouldering bodies of the creatures. Not one was left living after they were riddled with enough shots to kill them three times over or more.

"We did it," said Reynolds.

Kelly shook his head.

"That was just the beginning. They surely don't know our number. That's a scouting party sent in to test our strength."

"A scouting party? But they're all dead. How is that scouting?" Engel asked.

Kelly turned to see the Lieutenant was standing just three metres away, and he hadn't even noticed. She was in full battle attire and had clearly got in on the fight. He knew she shouldn't have, but he didn't have the heart to tell her that.

"They don't care about the individual. To their leaders,

the Mechs are just machines. Much like we see them. Mindless and soulless, a commodity to be used."

"And they keep doing as they're told? Why would they keep doing it? Why do they carry on going to their deaths?"

Kelly took a deep breath and sighed. Clearly, she had no understanding of the enemy they faced.

"Another day like this, and you'll stop asking why and simply stop caring," he replied.

"But they can't like this? They can't like going mindlessly about, dying at the wish of whoever leads them? Maybe they can be reasoned with, shown a different way."

Kelly laughed.

"One day, in a hundred years, and if the human race still exists, sure."

"But Taylor did it, didn't he? Everyone knows he did."

"Yeah, how did the Colonel manage it?" Reynolds joined in.

Kelly sighed once again. "Maybe it was a one in a million. Maybe there was some exceptional circumstance. Maybe Taylor is just one unique son of a bitch."

"Is? You think he's alive?"

"More and more everyday."

Kelly changed the magazine on his rifle and laid it in line with the others. He sat down with them. It felt remarkably comfortable, despite being a concrete floor. Nobody said a word now. They simply waited for the next assault. After a few minutes, they heard a call ring out.

"Hold your fire!" someone along the line ordered.

Kelly leapt up to look out through the slit. At first, he could see nothing and desperately looked in every direction to identify the source of the ruckus. Finally, he noticed a figure stagger into view from the north. It was human and walked as if either injured or having almost loss the will to keep going forward. His clothing was cut up and his head bare. The character's face was black from dirt and debris stuck to the skin. Finally, he stopped and looked up, and Kelly recognised Becker's face instantly.

"My god, he's alive!"

Kelly rushed out of the room and towards the main entrance. He hit the switch to open the blast doors, without even thinking of the dangers of doing so. He sprinted out to Becker and stopped just before him. He had expected the Captain to drop dead where he stood. He was covered in blood, but not much seemed to be his own. His face was burnt on one side and his uniform barely recognisable through the dirt and grime. Metal shards were embedded in his body armour.

"Are you okay?"

Becker looked at him with a blank expression.

"Are you hurt?"

Still nothing.

"Where is your platoon?"

He was silent for a few moments, then slowly opened his mouth and spoke in a croaky, dry voice.

21

"I have no platoon."

Kelly wrapped his arm around the Captain and led him inside the bunker where they were met by a medic. Kelly passed him over to the man who was joined by a woman helping out. As he was led away, Becker stopped and stared at Kelly.

"It's not enough, you know."

"What isn't?"

"To have to be killing them, as it's all we have to live for...there has to be more."

He turned and carried on, leaving Kelly with his chilling words. The Commander went back to the room where he had left Engel and Reynolds.

"Is he okay?" Reynolds asked.

"Looks like he has been through hell."

"We all have, Engel," said Reynolds.

Kelly didn't say a word, thinking more of what Becker had told him.

"How much longer do we have?" Engel asked, "Until they come again?"

Kelly finally snapped back to reality, his instincts cutting in. They needed a leader, and he knew he had to be the one.

"Not long now. That first wave was probably just a hunting party, enough to set a trap for Becker and discover our location. Now they'll send more."

"How many more?"

Kelly rubbed his chin, desperately wondering how to break the facts to them lightly, but decided it best to give it to them straight.

"More, and if we beat them, more again. And they'll keep coming until we run out of ammunition, till we are fighting in hand-to-hand. Until they have crushed us. That's how you deal with a resistance. Find it and crush it utterly."

It was a morbid overview of what they faced, but they knew it to be true. Thirty minutes passed without a sign of the Krys, but they were all aware they were out there. Finally, the signal came over the comms.

"Incoming aircraft."

The anti-aircraft weapons on the roof sprang into action. Return fire hit the rooftops of the bunker. They could hear the impacts, but the bastion all around them would not be broken. It was more like listening to heavy hail hit the roof of a house than a bombing raid.

"How long will that hold for?"

"I don't have all the answers, Lieutenant. It'll hold as long as it holds."

Becker suddenly appeared at the doorway. His uniform was still filthy, but at least his face had been washed. He had dozens of cuts over his face and neck but no serious injury. His eyes were quite different now. He still had the look of a man who'd suffered a great loss, but now that feeling was joined with a fiery hatred.

"If I'm going to die, it won't be in a field hospital while everything collapses around me," he stated.

He strode across the room and picked up one of the rifles Kelly had laid out. Kelly didn't want to press him; he was just glad to have him there. The gun emplacement beside him opened fire, and he turned sharply to see the first few Mechs land. He looked at Becker, who nodded back at him, took up position at one of the loopholes, and began systematically gunning down everything he could.

"Give them all you got!" Kelly hollered.

He followed in Becker's example and took aim, firing on as many as he could. He could barely believe the number of enemy who were falling to their guns. They seemed to drop like flies, and yet for everyone they killed, another dropped in to take his place.

"You keep coming!" Kelly bellowed, "You think we've been through hell! I'm gonna drag you right down there with me!"

He squeezed the trigger and fired like a mad man. There were so many targets he could barely miss. By the time his magazine was empty, less than twenty remained. He let go of the rifle and picked up the next, but as he took aim, he noticed something far larger descend into view. It landed hard and could barely support its weight.

It was a Juggernaut. He knew because Taylor had told him of them, and those stories alone were enough for him to realise how fearsome they were.

"Bring it down!"

He took aim more carefully now and fired for every potential weak point he could find. He hit the head but it did nothing. Next he aimed for the joints at the shoulder and then the groin. The heavy guns along the line joined him, as well as dozens of others, and finally the creature collapsed dead to the ground. He sighed in relief. But just as he thought they had gotten past this new danger, another two dropped in from above.

"Fire!"

They concentrated their fire on one as the two beasts stormed towards the blast doors. One was badly wounded before it got there, but the other hit the doors full force. To their surprise they survived the impact. They were relieved, but a moment later a large explosion rang out that buckled the doors inward. Kelly rushed to the corridor to look upon them and could see a metre-wide hole in the centre of the doors, where the creature had ignited like a living bomb. Through the hole he could see lines of Mechs advancing on them.

CHAPTER TWO

Taylor rolled uneasily in his bed. He'd barely slept in the time period he still called night. The clocks were set to GMT, and he was sticking to it, as was the fleet. As he tossed and turned, his elbow struck Parker who was squeezed in beside him. She groaned a little, but more from being awoken than hit.

"Oh, come on," she complained.

She looked her watch.

"Two hours? You kidding me?"

"You could always sleep in your own bed," he replied.

She wasn't sure if he was joking or not, but jabbed him in the side as she felt he deserved it either way. The clenched fist struck a rib, and he winced as it struck far harder than she'd intended.

"Sorry," she quickly added.

"No, it's okay. That's about the most excitement I've

had all week."

She laughed, but only briefly as she felt the same weariness.

"Think they'll ever get back to us?" she asked.

"We're sitting on their doorstep. Sure they will. What worries me is their response."

"But they fought with us once already?"

"Not through choice. It's pretty clear they are intimately familiar with the Krys. They have set up a life out here in peace. It's what we came out here to do, isn't it?"

She shrugged as if to agree in part.

"Well then wouldn't you be pretty pissed if some random race turned up with your old enemy in tow?"

She couldn't think of an answer, but they were soon interrupted anyway.

"Colonel Taylor to the bridge," a voice called over the comms, with no regard for the many still sleeping around them.

"News?" Parker asked.

"I doubt it. Probably just more bullshit."

He pulled on his BDUs and sidearm and carried on promptly. As he weaved his way through the corridors of the vessel, he could see the same dreary boredom mixed with anxiety that he felt inside, too.

This is getting old, he thought.

He reached the bridge to find himself being directed into the Admiral's quarters. He entered to find another six officers already sitting around the desk. Clearly, they had been there for some time. Before he could even stop with two feet together, Huber was hounding him with a question.

"Colonel Taylor, you think those things down there are spoiling for a fight, don't you?"

He could tell Huber had made up his mind, but he couldn't mindlessly go along with it.

"I wouldn't like to say, Admiral."

"Damn it, don't skate around with that nonsense. Give us your honest opinion, and don't hold anything back."

They all looked to Taylor and awaited his answer.

"Well...okay. I saw what tech this race has, just a little of it. I think if they wanted a fight, it would already be over, and we wouldn't be here to have this discussion."

"And what makes you think they just haven't made up their minds yet?" asked one of the other Captains.

He shrugged.

"They don't seem anything like the Krys. I don't think they'll harm us unless we present a danger to them."

"A danger? We've got a whole fleet parked in their backyard," replied Huber, "We have no chance to escape this place now. We are either going down there peacefully or with force, and if they make the first move, I want to know we are ready for it."

"Yes, Sir," Taylor replied.

"You seem unconvinced, Colonel?" Huber asked.

"Ball's not in our court, Sir. I'll fight to the very end if they come at us, but there is nothing more we can do than we are already doing."

"Not good enough, Colonel. I want your marines ready for assault around the clock. I want boarding teams prepared to assault any enemy vessels, and heavy weapons teams deployed at strategic locations around the ship. I want you to do your job, Colonel. You will liaise with the XO and ensure we are at full combat readiness for whatever might be thrown at us."

"Aye, aye, Sir," he responded.

"That will be all, Colonel."

Taylor turned and left quickly. He sighed as the door shut behind him.

"Waste of fucking time," he muttered to himself.

"What was that, Colonel?"

He looked up to see Vega had heard, but he wasn't going to repeat it.

Two hours later, he sat before a group of marines that had assembled for his briefing. A screen replayed video footage captured from the battle on the surface of the planet below. They had all seen it many times over, and that the new race of aliens possessed weapons and technology far more terrifying than they had encountered before. The video ended, and Taylor looked at them all as if waiting for some response.

"Well...questions?"

"Do we have any idea of their number?" Morris asked.

Taylor shook his head. "Your guess is as good as mine."

"So what are we training for?"

"The Admiral believes that if they decide against us, then they'll come for the fleet. If that happens, Parker, we do what we're here for. Internal defence and strategic boarding actions of enemy vessels."

Nobody said a word as they waited to hear how that would be achieved.

"Defence of the Washington has to be a priority, and to that end the Admiral will have me stay aboard to manage the defences. Captain King, I want you to assemble two boarding teams that are ready to deploy within five minutes, around the clock."

"For how long, Colonel?" he asked.

Taylor shook his head. "Until such time as something changes. Now, we already have double guard duties running, but the rest of you need to be ready to deploy just as quickly as Captain King, if not quicker. The simple reality is we don't know what technology this race has. Maybe they'll hit us up here, or maybe they'll force us into a ground battle."

The entire audience could hear the lack of confidence in Taylor's voice. He knew it would hit the already low morale, but he couldn't muster the strength to lie to them.

"You all know what you need to do. Let's get to it."

They groaned as they got to their feet and went about

their work. King came right at him and walked with purpose.

"I can organise these boarding parties, but we don't even know what we're facing. What kind of ships, their number, strength. We don't even know if we can breach their hulls. We're working on a lot of ifs and maybes here, aren't we?"

Taylor agreed with him. "And if I could have it any other way, I would. But this is the hand we have been dealt."

"All that we have given to get this far? You've kept up the fight when it seemed all hope was lost, but not now?"

Taylor had nothing left to say, and King could tell.

* * *

"More ammo! Get more ammo up here!" Kelly screamed.

He ran out of the room to check on the repairs to the main doors. Slabs of concrete lay scattered about the entrance, and sparks flew as three soldiers with welding guns installed reinforcements to the new patched up doors. They were welding everything shut. Nobody was under any illusions about what was going on the other side. Whatever happened, they would never be going out that way again.

Explosions rang out every few seconds from the Krys trying to pierce the bunker with heavy weapons. Kelly could feel the floor rumble beneath him on every impact. He turned and watched Engel struggling with a large ammo box under each arm. He rushed over and took one off her, but in doing so threw her off balance. She staggered against one wall and dropped the box. As it hit the round, the lid flew open where the clasp had not been fully sealed. Full magazines poured out over the floor.

Before Engel even had time to start recovering the magazines, there were six of their own people swarming her and grabbing as many as they could carry. Kelly went to the bunker door and dropped down his box, kicking it so that it slid into the centre of the room.

"Keep it up!"

He went to one of the loopholes to observe the fighting for himself. Mech bodies were strewn out across the yard, the whole width from the bunker to the rocks on the far side. They were knocking them down at an alarming rate from within the strong defences of the bunker, but they just kept coming.

"Will they never stop?"

He turned to find Engel standing by him. The look on her face was one of desperation. He shook his head.

"I can't imagine why. Never before have they ever shown mercy or willingness for peace. No, they'll keep coming until one side is destroyed."

"Then we lose?"

"We lost a long time ago, Lieutenant. I thought you

knew that. I believe I made that absolutely clear. All that we can do is what we are doing, right now. Killing as many of them as possible before the end."

A pulse ripped through the gun emplacement loophole and struck the heavy weapons team there. One of them was catapulted across the room from the power and struck the wall on the far side. Kelly rushed to the emplacement to take up the weapon without checking on the crew. He took aim and squeezed the trigger, but the shot ignited in the damage barrel and blew the weapon apart.

For a few seconds he was stunned and shocked. He was frozen in place, but then his eyes focused on the Mechs advancing on their position. He picked up his own rifle and started firing. At first, they were carefully aimed single shots, but that soon moved to bursts. As he slammed in a second magazine, there seemed little point in aiming any more as there was a wall of the enemy. He squeezed the trigger and held it down. The creatures were struck down one after another as dozens of rifles laid down continuous fire.

Then a gap opened in the line of creatures, and three Juggernauts rushed out, storming towards the doors. Kelly targeted his fire, and the others followed suit, but he knew they couldn't be stopped this time. A few moments later, two explosions rang out at the doorway. The floor rocked so violently, Kelly expected the roof to come down on top of them. A dust cloud passed over him as he got to his feet and rushed out to the entrance hall.

There was a metre-wide hole in the centre of the doors they had so recently repaired. Several of the soldiers nearby went forward to begin repairs.

"No! Get back!"

As Kelly said it, a pulse flew through the gaping hole and struck one of the soldiers square in the chest, knocking her flat onto the floor. The woman's armour was smouldering, and fragments had burned into her neck and shoulder, but she was alive. The huge hands of one of the Juggernauts reached into the weakened door and began prising it open like a tin can.

Kelly pulled two grenades from his webbing, primed them, and tossed them through the hole. He fired a few shots to follow them and then ducked away for cover. The grenades ignited with a fraction of the force and resonation of the weapons the enemy had used against the doors.

Just a few seconds later, Kelly was on his feet again.

"Fall back! Fall back!"

A few of the soldiers near him looked in surprise and for him to repeat the order. But as a pulse zoomed through the breach and flew past Kelly, they soon moved. He reached down for the wounded woman and hauled her to her feet.

"No time to lick your wounds, move!" he screamed at her.

Troops poured out from the bunker entrances either side of the hallway while he and Reynolds laid down fire through the breach. The flow of soldiers finally stopped long before he would have expected it to. The Commander leaned into the bunker that had been opposite theirs and could see the bodies of at least ten of their people. They had gotten it far worse than his position. He looked to each of the bodies to be certain there was no sign of life, but there was nothing.

"Kelly, we gotta move!" Reynolds pleaded.

He was suddenly tugged backwards, and the Captain hauled him out into the corridor. As he spun around, they both continued on into a quick paced charge to escape the incoming enemy.

"This isn't working!"

"You saw how many we killed, Captain! I'd say it worked rather well!" he answered.

It was the only justification he could think of for the losses they had endured.

They heard further explosions at their backs from the Mechs blasting their way in.

"At least we can bottleneck them now," he added.

"You really do try and find the positive in every situation?"

Kelly smiled.

"Somebody has to."

The corridor ahead broadened out into kill zone lines

of loopholes at two levels, and just one small doorway to one side that they headed for. They were the last survivors to make it. They went through it and found Corporal Berlin sealing the door. She didn't have to ask if they were the last; she knew Kelly would be the last one out.

He stopped, leaned against a wall, and took a deep breath.

"I'm getting way too old for this shit," he grumbled.

"Don't worry, you won't have time to age much further," a croaky voice replied.

He looked across the room. Becker was sitting on a worktop with a rifle in hand. His face had been hurriedly wiped of blood and dirt. Much of it was still ingrained in his hairline and neck. Kelly nodded in appreciation for having him there.

"So they haven't killed you yet?"

"They can shoot me, burn me, blow me up; they can fly motherfucking planes into me, but they can't kill me," he replied.

His voice was slow and weary as if he would pass out at any time. And yet he didn't.

Kelly dropped the magazine from his rifle and fed in a new one.

"You really are into this fighting to the very end?" Becker asked him.

Kelly looked up at him in surprise and then around to all those who surrounded them and listened in keenly.

"You never believed me, did you, none of you? I said this was the end, but you didn't believe it?"

Nobody responded.

"Yeah, well, maybe I didn't either. But what does it matter? We've lived on. We've gotten more out of life than most on this world. Every day we go on is a kick in the teeth to those bastards out there. They think of us as small and weak, an inferior race. But whose blood is running in rivers out there? Maybe death isn't all that bad. Maybe we were always destined to die against the never-ending hordes. But know that I am proud of you all. You fought on, and you fought well. If this is the end, then we will end it well."

He could see they appreciated the sentiment, but they couldn't bring themselves to cheer at the prospect of their own deaths. They could hear the resonation of the heavy Mech footsteps hurtling towards them now.

"You all know what to do. Fire at will!"

Kelly turned and positioned himself at one of the loopholes in the defensive line. There was no way over or around it. All the Mechs could do was come right at them and try and breach the walls. It was a purpose built killing zone for dealing with this very threat. As they waited for the first target, a dome-shaped object rolled into view. It looked like some kind of large grenade, but it stopped halfway into the kill zone.

"Cover!" Kelly shouted.

It was too late. The device opened and expanded rapidly, letting out a blinding ray of light over their entire position. Many of the troops winced in pain, dropping to the floor disorientated. Kelly had gotten to cover and was able to stay on his feet with at least a few others around him. He looked out through the loophole as one of the breaching Juggernauts stormed into view.

"Fire!"

His vision was blurred, but the creature was so large and coming right at them, he couldn't miss. He held the trigger down and opened fire as a dozen others joined him. He aimed low for its legs. After about twenty shots, he struck one of its knee joints and sent it hurtling face first to the floor. As it slid to a halt, they kept up their fire onto the top of its head and collar. More than two hundred shots were poured into the beast, when finally the explosive device it carried ignited. Kelly ducked back down for cover, just as a fragment of shrapnel flew through his loophole and embedded in the wall behind him.

Kelly was right back up on his feet and surveying the scene. There was a metre-deep crater in the floor where the creature had ignited, and only fragments of metal scattered about the area.

"Suicide bombers?" Reynolds asked, "All their wealth of technology, and that's the kind of primitive thing they come up with?"

"But it works, doesn't it? If you don't value the lives of

your soldiers, and they're either brave or stupid enough to do it, it's a cheap and simple means of getting the job done. We don't have any infantry in the world that could manage what those things can do. We'd have to bring in heavy armour or air strikes."

"But what do they fight for?"

Kelly shook his head. "I have no idea anymore."

"Here they come!" a voice yelled along the defensive line.

Three Mechs appeared at the entrance where the bottleneck opened up into the kill zone of their position. The second they appeared the first few shots rang out, and several others joined them. The creatures were cut down before they got more than two metres into the room. Kelly looked around to see crates of ammunition were being carried in, and he smiled at the realisation that it was their opportunity to butcher the enemy.

He left his people to keep up the onslaught and picked up handfuls of magazines, standing them on a ledge near his firing position. He casually reloaded and took aim. The Mechs began to topple over their dead, and yet continued coming forward like a swarm of ants.

Kelly took in a deep breath and then joined in the fire. He could feel the heat rise from the barrels of the weapons around him as they rattled off shot after shot. The Mech bodies began to amass at the bottleneck leading to the kill zone. There they formed a wall.

The gunfire slowed and finally came to a standstill. The heap of corpses had created a barrier between the two sides. The soldiers of the Drachenburg watched with anticipation to see the enemy's next move. Several took the opportunity to reload and then continue staring at the bizarre situation ahead of them. Kelly knew that any human being could not go on beyond that, but he also knew the enemy were nothing like them.

"Did we stop them?" Reynolds said quietly.

"Are you kidding me?" asked Becker, "You think a few bodies will stop them?"

As he said it, an explosion rang out, and the corpses were thrown forward into the open floor, blasting a breach into the corridor where fresh Mech warriors advanced. Kelly sighed, accepting the inevitable and raising his rifle to fire. A few seconds later, his finger was on the trigger without him even consciously intending to do so. Half the magazine was emptied before he even snapped out of the daydream, finding he had slipped into some kind of autopilot. He kept on firing until the magazine was dry and quickly ducked back down to reload.

Kelly looked over to Becker who was doing the same. He panned over to the doorway. Engel was struggling with yet more ammunition boxes full of grenades. He glanced back to Becker, who seemed to be the most sane and competent officer at his side, even if we was still suffering from the horrors of losing so many friends.

"They're never going to stop coming, are they?"

"No," Becker replied sternly, "Why would they stop coming? They didn't stop till they conquered the world, so why would they stop because a few of us are giving them some trouble?"

"And every day we live is a day we defy their conquest?"

Becker nodded in agreement.

"Then we have to leave."

Becker looked surprised.

"No fight to the end? No last man standing?"

"One day for sure, but not now. We escaped to this forest and we lived this long. We can do it again. We are going to die, no doubt, but not today."

Becker's interest seemed renewed.

"What do you have in mind?"

"Only really one way out of this now, Captain. The route we kept hidden from the moment we all arrived here. Pass the word. We're getting out of here."

Kelly turned to Captain Reynolds who had been listening in.

"I want two platoons to maintain this position until the rest are ready to move. And I want everyone else ready for that in fifteen minutes!"

"Fifteen?"

"Load as much food, water, and ammunition you can get in that time. Then get everyone wheels as fast as you can."

"Wheels?" asked Becker, "We have a lot heavier gear than that."

"We do, and that's for another job. Your job."

"Care to enlighten me on the plan?"

"Follow me, and it'll soon reveal itself."

* * *

Taylor stood with Jafar, looking at the heavily armoured suit of a Juggernaut in front of them.

"Well?" Taylor asked.

He was well aware they had done this very same thing before, and yet not found a satisfactory answer.

"Our heavy weapons will be able to take them on," added Morris.

"Yes, but they are in small numbers and far from flexible. We get to fighting in the corridors of the Washington, or one of the enemy vessels, and they could be taking us apart before we can bring the big guns to bear."

"Yeah, and it still doesn't change the fact these things are nothing like what we faced on that planet."

"No," replied Taylor, "but they are the closest thing we have to compare for size and power. If I could have recovered that robot...thing, whatever it was, I would have. So we focus our attention on what we do have. Our heavy weapons were needed to bring both of these monsters down effectively."

"We need them on our side," Parker joined in.

"I know that. We all know it, but it's out of our hands now."

"Surely they must see, Colonel. They must see we're in this together?"

"You can want it all you like, Morris, but it doesn't make it so. We don't know who these people are. We don't know what they want, what they have been through, or their connection to the Krys. Fact is; we don't know anything. So let's stop wishing, praying, and assuming. We're starting from scratch here. Look, listen, and observe. Maybe then we will learn something."

"Or get our heads blown off," Parker said quietly.

"Yeah, or that."

A voice came over the intercom, "Colonel Taylor to the bridge."

He shook his head.

Great, another opportunity to get shit heaped on my head, and be told to appreciate the fact!

He turned back to the group to see they awaited his instruction.

"All right, listen in. You all know this is bullshit. But if there is one thing we don't do, it's give up on our own people. Be ready."

"For what?" Morris asked.

"Anything."

With that, he turned and left. As he paced through the

corridors, he sighed, imagining what kind of grilling he would get this time. He was starting to wonder if he had just become Huber's punch bag. Taylor began to grumble under his breath but realising a few crew were taking notice, he stopped.

As he stepped aboard the bridge, he was once again ushered into the Captain's quarters, just as he had been so many times, but once inside, he soon found the tone was very different. He wasn't being called in there to be ribbed. He could tell they wanted something big from him.

"Colonel Taylor, please sit down," Huber said calmly.

Huber's tone was serious but not at all rushed or urgent. Taylor took his seat and now gave them his full attention. He was more curious than anything, but nobody said a word. Huber looked like he was trying to figure out a way to break some news to Taylor, but Mitch stayed silent and waited for it.

"Mitch..." the Admiral began.

First names terms, this is gonna be a big ask. Spit it out.

"Mitch, we've had contact from the ground."

"From them? The...whatever they are?"

Huber nodded.

"Okay, well that's a start. At least they aren't shooting. They want to join us?"

Huber shrugged.

"The message gave no indication of their intentions."

Taylor looked confused.

"Well what did they say?" he asked bluntly.

"The message was very short. It read, 'Colonel Taylor. Come alone to the co-ordinates we last met.'"

Taylor didn't know what to say.

"That's all, Admiral? That's the whole message?"

"Yes. We tried to respond and get some more information, but there has been nothing. The message couldn't be clearer. They want you and you alone."

"That's it? I get no backup? You've seen how dangerous those things are."

"According to you, Colonel, we have little chance against them, anyway. So risking your life down there alone is no worse than refusing to respond to their request."

Taylor grimaced, understanding how his own words were being used against him. He looked around at the other senior staff sitting about the room and could see that all they were waiting for, and all they were willing to accept, was for him to say yes.

He thought about it for a moment. The one thing he had always been able to rely on was his own people. The Inter-Allied, and the many friends and allies he had picked up along the way.

"Taylor, you know I wouldn't ask you to risk your life unnecessarily," Huber added.

Of course you would, Taylor thought.

But he knew he wasn't in a position to refuse, and he'd take any opportunity he could to get off the ship and onto solid ground.

"Colonel, I cannot order you to do this. Or at least, I can, but it wouldn't be fair. But I must stress the importance of this task, and you are the only one that can do it."

Taylor shook his head slowly and replied, "Okay, I'll do it, Admiral."

Huber sighed in relief.

"Good man."

"So no other stipulations? Nothing about weapons, or anything at all?"

"Nothing, but I suggest you go equipped as you were when you first met them. They are looking for some kind of consistency, so give it to them. And at least you'll be geared up for a fight, should you find one."

Alone and against the most advanced technology we have ever seen? Sounds appealing.

And yet he still felt comfort in knowing he would have a weapon to hand, even if it would do little to improve his chances.

"When do I set off?"

"They gave no indicator as to when, so we can only assume they meant as soon as possible."

Taylor stood up and started to leave.

"Colonel?"

He stopped and turned back to the Admiral.

"It is no secret that your woman is aboard."

"What of it?" Taylor answered, indignantly.

Huber looked surprised at his defensive response.

"Be sure to see her before you leave," he finally added.

Taylor relaxed, smiling in response at the Admiral's unexpected purpose.

"Aye, aye, Sir."

As he strode back towards Parker and the others, he thought about what Huber had just said. They both knew he was being asked to put his life on the line. Danger was nothing new to Taylor. But to face danger without a hope of fighting back, that was entirely alien and an unpleasant thought.

When he reached his own people, he stopped and could see Parker staring right back at him. She could see the expression on his face and instantly knew it wasn't news she was going to like. He approached slowly. The rest of his unit stopped what they were doing and turned their attention to him. He stopped before Parker and Morris. Jafar was there, too, looming over the humans.

"This is how it is. I've been called down to the planet. Alone. No pilot, no back up."

"No, you can't go without help," pleaded Parker.

Taylor shook his head.

"This isn't optional. You don't follow me. You do not leave this ship. Not any of you. This isn't what I want, but it is the way it has to be. You know what you have to do. Be ready for anything. Stay sharp, same as always."

"And if they strike you down?" Morris asked.

"Well then you better start worrying about this ship, as they'll surely be coming for you," he replied.

"Colonel Taylor, your ship is ready!" a voice called.

He looked over the flight deck to see a small fighter prepped for him. Rains was standing beside it, waiting for him. Taylor turned his attention to Parker. He laid his hand on her shoulder.

"You take care, Eli," he said quietly, his hand touching her cheek.

He turned and headed for the aircraft.

"You know you can't come with me, Rains."

"No, I'm with the programme. But I'll still be flying your ass," he replied and pointed to a remote console set up nearby.

"You might be alone, but I'll be flying you."

Taylor smiled. It was the best news he'd heard all day.

"All right. No time like the now, let's do this.

CHAPTER THREE

Taylor's craft soared towards the planet. He was sitting in the pilot's seat to get a full view ahead while everything was managed for him. He could tell Rains was flying, for nobody else was like him, but it did feel strange.

"Colonel, you see that big red button at your two o'clock?" Rains asked over the comms.

"Yeah, I see it."

"That's your get out of Dodge button. If I lose remote control, or for any reason you want to get the hell out, you press that button, you hear? It'll return you to the Washington and land you safely. It won't be as fast as me, and it won't be able to do anything fancy, but it will get you home okay."

"Home? I wish you had a button for that."

"Hey, you wouldn't want to go there anyway. It's probably crawling with alien assholes."

Taylor could not help but laugh, but he was soon silenced as he visualised that sight. Mechs occupying his home was a depressing thought that only served to stack onto the increasing depression they were all suffering from.

"You really think you can convince these sons of bitches to join up?" Rains asked.

He realised the Lieutenant was clearly of the same mind.

"I'll do what I can, same as always."

"You need us, you call, you hear?"

"What do you mean?"

"I mean Captain King is ready to assault any target at a moment's notice. You send us the word, and the cavalry will be en route."

Taylor took in a deep breath and slowly responded.

"Listen to me. I don't care what happens down there, you don't come after me, got that?"

"But..."

"No buts, that's an order. I won't have war started with another race just because of me. You will not let that happen, you hear me?"

There was no reply for a moment and finally a sigh, and then, "Got it."

Eddie went silent now as they made their descent onto the planet. It was a dry and craggy land, broken up with wide expanses of flat desert. He couldn't decide if it reminded him of Nevada or North Africa, but neither were places he was keen to see again.

He could see the base up ahead. It remained unchanged from the last time he had arrived there. There was no sign of life in sight. Not a single vehicle of either race.

"I'm putting you down here, a hundred metres north of the facility," said Rains.

"All right, then. Thank you and maintain radio silence from now on, unless I break it."

"You got it. Good luck, Colonel."

Eddie brought him in on a quick, but supremely well controlled descent, and landed just as he had said. The landing gear touched down, and the engines powered down in seconds. Absolute silence followed.

It feels like being inside a sealed box, he thought.

But when he hit the door release, and opened the vessel to the elements, he found it was just as silent outside.

Loneliness was not something he was accustomed to, nor craved, but neither had either ever given him cause for concern, until now. Now he felt cold inside. He didn't want to move. He couldn't bring himself to get out of his seat and place one foot in front of the other. He looked at the big red button that would 'send him home' as Rains had put it.

It's not home, but going back to Eli Parker and my comrades is the next best thing.

"Why did it have to be me?" he asked himself out loud,

"Of all the fools that it could have been, why is it always me?"

He finally mustered up the will to stand, finding he had to tell himself over and over what to do, to walk and to breathe. Not a fibre of his body wanted to do a thing. He grabbed his rifle from the rack beside him and eventually made his way to the door. He took in a breath of the air, and that at least had a calming effect.

"Nothing else in the world like it."

He had to keep talking to himself to at least maintain his sanity, and real air helped a lot. He jumped from the doorway and felt his feet land on dry, hard ground. He looked around with suspicion, expecting to be attacked any moment. The only relief he felt was that at least he was not dealing with the Krys. He knew that whoever this race was, they seemed nothing like their sworn enemy. He didn't know what drove them or what their sensibilities or morals were, but they at least seemed to have some. He attached the sling swivel to his armour and let the rifle hang at his side, with just his right hand on the grip. He wanted to appear casual and friendly, without actually being vulnerable. He carried no shield, for he didn't want to give the impression he had come for a fight.

He strolled towards the town as if he were taking a walk in the park. He had to focus all the energy he had on appearing casual and friendly, and that meant fighting his instincts. He was approaching an urban environment with endless opportunity for ambush.

"Where the hell are they?" he muttered to himself.

He reached the edge of the facility to find empty boxes and clothing strewn about where it had been left in a hurry. A very light breeze rustled a sheet on the ground, but nothing seemed to have moved from where it was left a month before. It was a ghost town. He had suspected as much, but had still hoped there would at least be a greeting party awaiting his arrival.

"Come on, where are you? Don't tell me this was all just to stick the knife in," he grumbled.

He thought he heard footsteps to his flank and stopped dead, snapping his head around to look for any signs of movement in the building he was passing. His right hand took a firmer grip on his rifle, but he fought the urge to raise it to his shoulder. He was frozen solid, watching and listening for any sign of movement, but there was none. He wasn't sure if his mind was playing tricks on him now.

Mitch carried on down the road in and finally took a turn into the main square of the complex. It was a broad open space with buildings on all sides and a few abandoned ground vehicles. There was no sign of life. He strolled out toward the centre of the area. It reminded him of his days of fighting in the arena. He reached it and rotated around, looking in all directions.

"Where are you?" he asked.

Still silence.

"Where are you!" he yelled at the top of his voice so that it echoed around the buildings.

He turned and turned, finally coming to a stop when he saw a single one of the aliens standing ahead of him. He gasped in surprise.

"Where the hell did you come from?" he asked rudely.

It looked like the same one he had spoken to before, but it was hard to tell for sure. The creature's face appeared to show no emotion at all, and its skin was such a matte charcoal black that it barely reflected any light at all so that picking out features was difficult. He took his time to study its form, just as he had done before. It surprised him that it was of humanoid form, just as the Krys were.

This race was smaller and slighter than the Krys. They had an air of sophistication about them that led him to believe they were a people more of the mind than the body. It felt as if he had been studying the creature for a full minute without a word from it. He expected more of them to arrive any moment, but nobody came.

"I am Colonel Taylor. You sent for me?" he finally asked politely.

"I know who you are, Colonel."

"Can I know your name?"

The creature looked surprised. It was the first sign of emotion he had seen, and that surprise turned to an almost uncomfortable reluctance.

"Can't really have much of a conversation if I don't

even know who I'm talking to, can I?" Taylor asked.

He could see the creature was thinking about his question and did not waste any words.

"My name is Irala."

"Okay, and what is your...rank? Title? What is it you do here?"

"I am here to give you our answer."

Not quite what I had in mind, Taylor thought.

But he didn't press the matter; he decided instead to try and get in the first word to ensure he got the answer he wanted.

"So you've fought them before? The Krys?"

No response came.

"Irala you said your name was? Well, Irala, we call those things we fought the Krys. What do you call them?"

"I will not repeat their name here on our own world."

Taylor nodded in agreement. He could understand that.

"So you have fought them before?"

He could tell the creature was very intelligent, and yet it simply observed and watched him and said as little as possible.

"You sure seem to hate them," he added.

"Hate?" Irala, appearing confused.

He seemed to think on it for a while, or at least Taylor assumed it was a he. The voice was deep and strong.

"The reaction you had to first seeing one of them, even though he was among us," added Taylor, "That is a kind of hatred that runs deep to the core. I know that hatred because it runs pure in my veins."

"And yet you still stand beside one of them?"

Finally!

He had at last drawn some response from the creature and felt he was getting somewhere.

"It was by sheer accident that one came to be my friend. Jafar is his name. And I say he is the reason I now stand here, and hope there is some chance we can be allies. You don't know me. I don't know you. I am not asking for us to be friends. I only ask that we fight a mutual enemy together."

Once again Irala seemed to struggle with the concept, as if he wanted to agree but was unable to.

"Come on. You hate them. I hate them. They stole our world and exiled us from it. I bet they did something much the same to you, didn't they?"

The creature nodded.

"This world can't be yours, so little populace and development. I don't believe you came from here. My bet is they drove you to this planet. Same reason we have ended up here. Am I right?"

"Yes," Irala replied abruptly.

"So you know what we're dealing with. You know the shit storm that we faced. We survived it for years. Years are a long time for us. I killed Erdogan's own blood, Demiran, with my own hands."

Taylor noticed Irala's eyes light up just a little at the sound of the names.

"You killed Demiran? In personal combat?"

Taylor smiled; pleased he had touched on a nerve.

"Yes…yes I did. I fought him on our own world, with my own hands against his. Nothing but bladed weapons, and I struck him down and drained his blood on the sands of the desert in a place not so dissimilar to this."

Irala seemed glad to hear the news and at least relieved in some way.

"So you knew him? Demiran?"

Taylor knew he had to keep pressing the alien to get him onside, and press he did.

"So he crapped all over you, too? Don't hold back. He nearly made my people extinct. So come on, share with me. We have a saying on my planet. 'The enemy of my enemy is my friend.' Is that not where we're at?"

"Demiran. We were greatly offended by him. I was greatly offended. News of his death brings relief, if it is true."

Taylor scowled at the creature.

"You question my honesty? My integrity? I am a Colonel of the United States Marine Corps. I am Mitch Taylor of the Inter-Allied Regiment. My word if fact, and any man who would say otherwise is not my friend."

The creature didn't seem offended but more curious as to his sudden change in demeanour.

"Will you stand there and call me a liar?" Taylor asked, "Because if you do, you and me are gonna have a problem."

He unclipped his rifle, let it drop to the ground, and drew his Assegai, but the creature did nothing. He couldn't tell if it was unsure or just curious. He had seen their power and knew what a threat they posed, but he could see a change of approach was needed, even if that meant risking everything.

"So?" Do we have a problem?"

Irala seemed amused by his question and utterly relaxed.

"If you killed the Lord Demiran, I would know how so that my family can revel in the fact. We suffered a tremendous loss at his hands."

"All this technology and power, and you were not able to kill him yourself?"

"We are few, and they were many."

"Yes," replied Taylor, "And sometimes no matter how good you are, and how hard you fight, it isn't enough. This is how we got out here to begin with."

Irala seemed to agree and understand but moved little more than his eyes. Taylor could see he was getting somewhere. He was tapping into a hatred that ran deep, and he felt it, too.

"But they are far fewer now. We might have lost the war and our planet, but they paid a dear price for it. You may be few, and we are few. But together we could be strong enough to..."

"To what?" Irala interrupted.

Taylor paused for effect and to reel the alien in.

"To win," he finally said, barely any louder than a whisper.

Irala was silent and clearly thinking deeply about what he was hearing.

"You know we can do it. We have a shot. Or we just get chased round the universe and hunted down till all of us are dead."

"Colonel Taylor. I am here to inform you of our answer."

Shit!

He knew he had lost his attention. He knew he was close to getting him on side, but he didn't want to be as rude as to interrupt.

"We will not enter your war, nor do we perceive you as an enemy. However, your presence here brings unnecessary danger to this world, and we insist that you leave and do not come back."

Taylor shook his head.

"How? How can you let us go to our deaths, knowing those bastards will only come for you when you too stand alone?"

"We have lived here peacefully for longer than you have drawn breath, and probably generations before you."

Taylor thought it curious that the alien seemed to have an understanding of the human life span in comparison to his own, and that got him thinking.

"You've seen us before, haven't you? You knew of the existence of humanity?"

Irala said nothing, but Taylor could tell by his lack of response that he was hitting the nail on the head.

"Then you must have been to our world. You must have seen it? Oceans and forests for as far as you can see."

He kicked the sand beneath his feet.

"A place like this on Earth is the kind of shithole that is easily avoided. I mean no offence, but hell you can do better than this. I'm betting your own world wasn't anything like this dusty hell?"

Irala blinked his eyes as if in some kind of recognition, the first time Taylor remembered him doing so.

"So no. We're not asking to live here with you. I'm asking you to help us take back our world, Earth, and for us to live there together. God knows there's enough room for both our races since the wars have devastated our population."

"I am sorry, Colonel, but we have made our decision."

"So all this time we've been waiting. All this time you've stood here and exchanged niceties with me, and it was all for nothing?"

"We have met. We have exchanged words, and we part without conflict. What is the problem?"

"The problem is you aren't seeing sense or logic. You send us packing, and we're dead. Ever since Erdogan turned up, we've been fighting a losing war. Sure we might last a few more weeks or months. Maybe we'll even get a few years on the run. But he'll find us and he'll kill us all. I want my planet back, and the only way that's gonna happen is if we work together."

"We have made our decision," Irala replied sternly.

Taylor could see he was wasting words and time now. He turned to walk away and got a few paces before stopping and looking back. He was angry now and couldn't contain himself.

"Is there nothing that will make you see sense? Is there nothing that will change your mind?"

No response came.

"Then fuck you for wasting my time. Fuck you for leaving us to die. You just handed Erdogan his final victory."

Taylor didn't wait for a response and doubted he would get one anyway. He turned back and stormed off back towards his transport. As he did, he cursed and spat, and voiced his anger to himself. He was fuming and wanted nothing more than to hit something. He reached the ship, climbed aboard, and slumped into the pilot's seat.

"Goddamn aliens! Useless."

He reached for the console and opened a channel.

"This is Colonel Taylor to the Washington."

Just a few seconds later a response came, and it was the Admiral himself. It was clear the bridge crew had been waiting silently for his call. It was obvious to everyone how important his mission was.

"This is the Washington. You okay, Colonel?"

"Yeah, ready to come on home," he said with a sigh.

"Do you need further assistance down there, Colonel?"

"Negative. They want us off this world and out of here."

In those few short words, he had explained all there was to say.

Why couldn't that alien asshole break it to me simply? he asked himself.

"All right, Colonel, come on home," came the response, "I'll have you put through to your pilot."

Taylor could hear the immense disappointment in Huber's voice. Knowing they weren't going to have to fight should have been a relief, but they both knew it only meant a more prolonged battle to the end against Erdogan. Eddie's overly excited voice came over the comms once again.

"Colonel, what's going down? Glad to hear you're still breathing."

"Yeah, I'm still here."

"So how'd it go?"

"Well, put it this way, I'll be the last human to ever step foot on this dusty piece of a shit planet."

"That well, huh?"

Taylor couldn't help but smile.

"How do you stay so goddamn chirpy, no matter what?"

"How are you always such a badass?" he responded.

Taylor couldn't think of a response, but he got the idea.

"So what, this is the way we're born? I was born to slug it out fighting every asshole across the galaxy, and you were born to be a wise cracking cheery son of a bitch?"

"Sounds about right."

"Well, okay then, nice to know some things never change."

"Consistent and steadfast, that's me."

"Just get me out of here," replied Taylor.

"You got it."

The engines began to power up.

"You know we really..."

Eddie's voice was interrupted by a loud crack that echoed through the speakers of the craft, and then the feed went silent.

"Eddie? Rains? You there?" Taylor asked.

No response. He was getting anxious now as the engines powered down, and he knew the remote access had been lost.

"Rains?"

There was still no response. Now Taylor was really starting to worry. He reached forward and punched the big red button that would send him home. He waited for just a few seconds, and nothing happened.

"Oh, come on!" he yelled.

He smashed his fist down on the button once more and just as it connected, the engines fired up. He realised he was being impatient, but he couldn't help it.

"Come on, you piece of junk, let's move!"

He felt the power surge as they lifted off the ground, but at a snail's pace compared to how Rains would have done it.

"Move, move, move!" he shouted.

He knew it would get him nowhere, but he could not contain himself. He gripped his rifle and held it close; knowing all he could do was sit and wait. He opened another channel to the Washington.

"This is Colonel Taylor to the Washington, please come in."

No reply came, so he repeated the same message. Still nothing. He sat back now and just waited. It seemed to take an age to get to the edge of the atmosphere, and he watched nervously for the first glimpse of space. Never before had he been so eager to get into space.

"Please be nothing, please be nothing," he muttered to himself over and over. But he knew deep down that something was up. The atmosphere began to thin, and he got a first blurred glimpse of what he was heading for. He could just make out flashes of light, orange and yellow patches of light in the distance. He couldn't focus yet or workout what he was seeing.

Then finally he broke orbit, and the view cleared up.

He gasped at the fearful sight before him. The fleet was being bombarded by constant fire from more Krys vessels than he could count, and at the centre of them Erdogan's own ship. The very same ship they had fought so hard to disable when they escaped from Earth. He was instantly hit with flashbacks of the way the alien Lord had thrown him about like a ragdoll.

"My god," he whispered.

He got up to the edge of his seat and tried to think of something to do, but he knew there was nothing. His shuttle was making its way back at a leisurely and casual pace. He looked out and could see the Washington was being hit by shot after shot. Pulses were ripping holes in its hull and assault craft were heading her way.

Taylor shook his head. "This must be the end. This is what it must look like," he said to himself.

Above all else, he was furious he wasn't there aboard the flagship to go down with her. A number of other vessels stood alongside her and were giving as much back to their attackers as they could. The rest of the fleet were on course for the planet. Taylor knew Irala's people could well fire on them, but it was a better chance of survival than facing the Krys.

Huge pulses of light burst from Erdogan's ship, the Fatihi, and tore the hull from the Washington as if she were a tin can, and yet she kept firing. He was drawing closer to the remainder of the fleet now and passed alongside the vast barges that housed the only known survivors of the human race.

Taylor watched the battle rage for fifteen minutes. It was like seeing a frigate duel as the vast ships battled it out. He could see they had no chance, and Huber must have known it. It was clear he was merely trying to buy the rest of the fleet enough time to reach the planet. Every single person he cared for in life was in the battle, and he was helpless as he watched them being torn apart. His shuttle was still making its way to the fight, but he was still a few minutes out, and he wondered if he'd even get past the gunfire. He slid the visor shut on his helmet to seal his suit, knowing there was a good chance he'd need his own air.

"This is your end," a growly voice said behind him.

He almost leapt out of his skin and jumped from his seat with his rifle at the shoulder. Erdogan stood there, and it sent a shiver down his spine. He knew there was no chance it could be his real physical presence, but he wanted to be sure. He drew his combat knife and launched it at the alien. The blade passed right through and bounced clumsily off the wall behind him.

Taylor was relieved to find it was a hologram, as he had suspected. Erdogan didn't move, and he carried no weapons. He stood upright, looming over Taylor. His head almost reached the roof of the crew compartment, and he carried himself with arrogance.

"What do you want from me?" Taylor asked.

"Your life...but not until you have watched your people die. I want it to be the last thing you ever see."

Taylor could think of no witty response, and neither did he want to. He turned away and slumped back in the pilot's seat as if he were a broken man.

"You could never win," added Erdogan, "You struggled to overcome the lesser of my kind. You barely made it through. And when met with a real enemy, you died in your masses and ran like the weak cowards you are."

Taylor tried to ignore him, but he could still feel his heart pounding. Initially, it was from the surprise of Erdogan's voice, but now it was from bitter hatred. Out of the corner of his eye, he caught a glimmer of movement at the side of the cockpit window and turned to look. A rippling effect seemed to pass him by, and then another. He could not tell the size or distance of these anomalies.

"What the hell?"

Several more passed all around him, and they were heading right for the battle. They seemed almost translucent and appeared to flicker and blur the sight of space ahead. He counted more than a dozen of the objects heading right for the fight. He squinted to try and make out what they were, when finally one of the objects opacity faded and revealed itself. A vessel like nothing he had ever seen before. It was almost matt black and blended well against the space beyond. Only the flashes of the pulse weapons and explosions on the ships were lighting up its silhouette for him to see. A single engine on the back of the vessel emitted almost no light, and they moved at a rapid pace. The vessel was long and pointed at the bow, almost fish-shaped.

Taylor turned and looked back to see if Erdogan had reacted to what he was seeing, but the alien was nowhere to be seen.

"Go on, do it!"

He was well aware nobody could hear him, but he didn't care.

"Do it! Kill them!" he cried.

A beam suddenly burst from the mysterious vessel and extended out to one of the medium-sized vessels fighting beside the Fatihi. The beam cut through the enemy craft as if with no resistance at all, and then exited on the far side until it cut the ship in two. The crew and contents of the vessel were sucked out into space as the ship parted cleanly into two almost perfectly proportioned halves.

"Fuck me," Taylor murmured in awe.

As he spoke, several of the rest of the camouflaged vessels revealed themselves and opened fire as the first had done, with an array of different weaponry from beam weapons to pulses, and rapid fire cannons that emitted vast surges of pulse-like volleys. Three of the Krys vessels were obliterated in the opening volley, but they soon turned to oppose this new threat.

Taylor watched in amazement as this third force ploughed into the battle, and an apocalyptic battle ignited before his eyes. A dozen other human vessels had turned back from the barges to join the fight, having seen they now had a chance. Empty hulks floated about space, and fighters from all sides zoomed all around. He was close to the Washington when he saw massive explosions burst out from her hull. The pulses kept striking her, and he watched in horror as the upper hull buckled, and a large hole opened up. He could just about see the shape of crewmembers being sucked out through the breach.

"No!" he screamed.

He looked around for something to do, for someway to help, but there was none. He watched several craft fly out from the landing bays, and many more escape pods followed them. He prayed his friends had made it out alive. Pulses continue to hit the Washington relentlessly. What guns and missile systems she still had operational continued to fire, but it was the end for her.

Then Taylor found he had a new problem of his own. His shuttle was still en route to a ship that was likely to explode at any minute. He looked at the controls and tried to make some sense of them.

"Come on, can't be that difficult," he told himself.

He had watched Rains do it by muscle memory alone so many times; he imagined it was little more than like riding a bike. But the three consoles around him had a blinding array of switches and gauges. There were two joysticks in front of him. He grabbed one and tried to alter course with it, and then the other, but to no avail. He couldn't even see any way of taking over from the autopilot that he had activated. He looked back to the burning wreck of the Washington, and still it was taking fire as dozens of small ships and shuttles fled for their lives.

"Ah, hell!" he yelled.

He rushed to the side door of the shuttle and pulled the emergency release catch so that the door blasted off into space. He took one look outside and jumped. He was used to jumps within Earth's gravity, but this had a very different effect. He continued on towards the Washington. Mitch quickly fired the thrusters on his suit and put them to full power, pointing at the hulk. His ascent towards the vessel finally slowed, and just as his power ran out, he began to move slowly away from her.

There was nothing he could do now but turn around and watch the battle continue as he floated very slowly back the way he had come. An escape shuttle that was about to zoom past him exploded, hit by a pulse, and two small parts of debris from it smashed into him. He covered his face to protect his mask. He just had to hope his armour would protect his mechanical compression suit beneath it.

The debris bounced off him and did little to affect his course. He looked down to check his equipment. A deep gash had cut into the torso plate of his armour. It was the thickest armour on his body, and probably the only place that would have saved him. But he wasn't thinking of himself any longer. A huge flash lit up inside the Washington, and explosions erupted out of new holes that were blown out of the outer hull. The last of the lights and engine power faded, and she was finally gone for good. Taylor raised his hand in a casual salute to her.

"You did us proud, and far more than we could have asked for," he said, as if speaking at a close personal friend's funeral. It seemed the beginning of the end. But then he turned his attention to their allies. The battle was still far from over, and what remained of the humans were still fighting and battling on.

CHAPTER FOUR

Almost fifteen minutes had gone by as Taylor watched the battle unfold. His boosters had largely recharged from the solar energy that was in abundance. He checked his air supply and was content it was at an acceptable level, but he looked around for any way of getting either in or out of the battle rather than watching from the sidelines, which was both dangerous and useless.

He looked back towards the planet that the barges were reaching and knew that if he used some boost, he could likely make it, but watching the apocalyptic battle he realised he couldn't leave. There were more than thirty ships on either side battling it out now, with almost as many floating as empty hulks. He knew that even if the Inter-Allied forces still remained, he had no chance of finding them, so he looked for something recognisable and some place he could be of use.

Looking around for some point of entry into the battle, he saw one of the enemy fighters crash into the lower hull of the French Heavy Cruiser, the Diderot, where Major Moye was based. A few seconds later, one of the enemy heavy assault craft hit the breach and burst through, in what seemed a calculated assault. Taylor knew this was his chance. He hit his boosters and fired towards the breach in the cruiser's hull. Fighters weaved in and out around him, and it was sheer luck alone that he wasn't hit. As he closed the distance, he found he was slightly off course and tried to redirect, but it was too late.

Taylor slammed into the hull a metre off the breach, but he held on with one hand to a ribbing in one of the plates of the hull. He hit his boosters just a little, and it provided the forward motion to get him to the breach to manoeuvre in. As he did so, his grav boots locked onto the deck he was entering and allowed him to walk almost as if in normal gravity.

"Time for some payback," he whispered.

He looked around for any sign of the enemy to strike down, but there was nothing. He carried on to the edge of the room where the blast doors had sealed and found a decompression chamber. The security had been overridden, and it was open for anyone to pass through. He stepped inside and waited for it to pressurise. He stood wondering what he would find on the door the other side, and he had only one thought.

I wish I'd brought my damn shield.

The door opened, and his rifle was at his shoulder ready to fire, but he did not find the enemy. He was met with the bodies of five French Navy crew scattered about the corridor. Not a single Mech lay dead amongst them. There was no sign of weaponry, and it was obvious they had been taken by surprise. Two stretchers lay there with them; it looked as if they had been carrying wounded. He shook his head. He had fully expected to find casualties, but to see they had not even been armed and able to put up a fight made him feel sick.

He carried on and took a bend, finding five Mechs dead and three marines with them. As he stepped cautiously past the bodies, he heard a groan from one of the marines and knelt down to check for a pulse. As he did, he felt movement and so helped the man roll over. It was Moye himself. He was cut and bleeding on his left arm and looked like a train had hit him. He mumbled in French, and for all of Taylor's time in the country, he couldn't understand anything he said.

"Major?" Taylor asked.

He kept his voice low and shook Moye, trying to wake him up fully. Finally, he stopped mumbling and looked at Taylor's face, clearly recognising him.

"What happened? How did you even get here?"

"How doesn't matter. You've been boarded. Looks like they ran right through you."

The Major looked at the bodies around him.

"Yes, one of the big things. I think you call them Juggernauts."

Taylor shook his head.

"That's the last thing you want aboard."

"It's not like we haven't seen them before."

Taylor took his hand and hauled him to his feet. He winced in pain but was at least able to support his weight. The rifle slung at his side was snapped in two where he must have landed on it after being struck by the Juggernaut. He unclipped it and reached down to take one from his dead comrades, with no second thought. Taylor often forgot how much experience and combat everyone else had seen beside him. He knew that if Moye had made it this far in life, he must have at least some good qualities.

Taylor reached down and took one of the shields from the bodies. Moye picked his own up.

"They'll be heading for the bridge. They always do," said Taylor.

"I know, and we don't have long to stop them. If we can stop them at all."

"Lead the way."

They carried on alone. Two officers without any support at all. They both knew how desperate the situation was, but neither was willing to say it or let it affect them in doing their jobs.

"You saw the Washington go down?" Moye asked

quietly.

"Saw it with my own eyes."

"Then I am sorry."

"Sorry for us all. She was as important to me as she was to us all."

"But your unit?"

"They either died doing their jobs, or they managed to get off before she went down. Nothing more I can do by worrying about them."

It was the kind of logic he always spouted to keep spirits up, but he still didn't believe it himself, and Moye gave him a bemused look that suggested he knew it.

Then they heard gunfire up ahead, but it was not coming from friendly weapons. The two officers continued on with their shields held out before them and trigger fingers ready to fire in an instant. They came into sight of the enemy. Their backs were in plain view, and neither gave them a chance to fight fair, opening up on fully automatic and cutting down two of the Mechs in the opening burst. Three more turned to return fire, but it was too late for them. They kept their fingers on the triggers until they were relentlessly cut down.

Neither of them stopped going forward as they changed out their magazines, and Moye led the way to the bridge. They passed the bodies of a dozen Mechs and more than three times their number in crew. At last they heard the familiar sound of Reitech rifles firing. Moye peered around a corner from where they could hear the sound and saw a group of marines dug in at an intersection and defending a single flank. He shouted something in French and followed it with his name before stepping out towards them. He spoke a few words and got several sentences back. Moye looked back to Taylor as if expecting input.

"In English?" Mitch asked.

"We've got multiple hull breaches and at least three boarding actions reported."

"They'll still be going for the bridge," he replied.

Moye ordered the marines to stay put, and led Taylor onwards. They would have appreciated some support, but they had to cover more ground than they would together.

"What will they do if they reach the bridge?" Moye asked.

"Kill the crew, turn any weapon systems still active on our own fleet, and likely attempt to ram the nearest one of ours."

"So if they take it, we're finished?"

Taylor nodded.

"Then let's not let that happen."

"Indeed."

"And that Juggernaut? What if it reaches the bridge?"

"I've got a couple of ideas on that."

"Want to share?"

A pulse struck the wall on their left, and they ducked down, returning fire from behind their shields at the single

Mech advancing on them. Taylor felt one of the pulses impact on his shield. As it splashed white-hot matter across the surface, the debris hit the barrel of his rifle. One of the Reitech shots soared down the barrel and jammed in the bottleneck created by the pulse damage, blowing the barrel apart. Shrapnel from the barrel embedded in the front and rim of the shield. It was all that saved it from coming right for his face.

"Fuck!" he yelled.

"Come on, Colonel!"

Taylor unclipped the wrecked weapon and dropped it to the deck, drew out his Assegai, and ran after the Major. He knew they were likely running to their deaths, but it was far better than dying out in space with nobody to fight at all.

"The bridge is just up ahead," said Moye.

They rushed up a short flight of steps and found three Mechs and the Juggernaut standing at the entrance to the bridge. One of the creatures had a device connected to the door locking mechanism and was overriding it. As Taylor and Moye came into sight, the huge blast door lock mechanisms opened and the door rose, revealing the bridge.

The four aliens blocked off much of the view to the bridge, but they could just about see the faces of a few of the crew and the Captain. They were like rabbits in a spotlight, and Taylor could fully understand why. The

Captain shouted something to one of the crew. He reached for the emergency release of the blast door, but as he went for it, the Juggernaut stepped inside and grabbed his neck and snapped it single-handed.

"Go!" Moye screamed.

They rushed at the Mechs. They had turned to face them to allow the Juggernaut to go about its work of devastation. Moye was firing on full auto, and the first creature was riddled with more than twenty shots by the time they reached them and dropped where it stood. Moye ducked under the pulse cannon of the second and drove his shield up, forcing the weapon to go vertical before placing his gun barrel into the creature's gut, riddling it with eight shots.

Taylor smashed the other's weapon aside with his shield with such force, it caused the creature to turn and stumble towards him. His Assegai drove deep into its collar until it ran up to the hilt. He turned aside and allowed the body to fall past him and stepped onto the bridge.

The Juggernaut had just stamped on one of the crew and crushed her to death. Several others fired at it with pistols, but they had no effect at all. The creature didn't seem at all bothered. Moye took aim and emptied the last of his magazine into its back. The final few shots made it spasm slightly, as if some of them had at least hurt the beast.

It spun around to face this new threat. Moye drew out

his Assegai, and he and Taylor put some distance between themselves, preparing to fight it hand-to-hand.

"Ever taken one of these down?"

"Not without help, Major."

"You've got me."

"I meant rather more help."

The beast finally rushed at Moye, being the one who had hurt it. It swung for him, and he parried the strike off and spun off to its flank, trying to stab at the beast, but the impact of the parry had pushed him too far off to the side. Taylor stood at the doorway to the bridge, and it was coming right for him. He stood his ground confidently as if with no fear at all.

Wait, wait, wait! Taylor cautioned himself.

The Juggernaut was almost on him when he quickly ducked down and smashed his shield full force into its lower legs with all the strength he could muster. The beast's legs went out from under it. It went forward into a dive, hitting the deck, and scraping along it for two metres before finally coming to a halt in the doorway.

But Taylor was already on his feet and wasn't going to give the beast a second to recover. He leapt to the emergency door shut button and smashed it with his hand. The beast was just rising at the waist when the half-metre thick door plunged down into the creature's torso, almost cleaving it in two, and pinning it to the deck. It writhed for just a few seconds, finally falling silent.

Taylor hit the door button again, and it opened up to reveal the gaping wound in the creature's chest where the door had crushed its armour into its own flesh. But that wasn't enough of a reassurance for Taylor. He knelt down beside it and drove his Assegai deep into one of the openings in the wrecked armour. As he drew it out, blue blood seeped from the weapon. He turned back to see Moye watching in amazement.

"Was that really your idea? Jam it in the blast door?"

"Yes, sort of."

"You know how crazy that was? How little chance there was of you pulling that off?"

"Yeah, a lot better than we had fighting it."

Moye couldn't disagree and looked at the corpse of the Juggernaut. They both turned to the ship's Captain. He stood like a statue in total shock.

"Captain?" Taylor asked, "Captain!"

He slowly looked at Taylor.

"Get this ship back in the fight!"

He seemed to snap out of his daydream state and turned to his crew, bellowing a stream of orders. Taylor was suddenly aware of the projection there showing what was happening. With his attention entirely focused on the Juggernaut, he had not even noticed the space battle going on around them. He took his time to study what was going on now and could see the battle was far from decided.

"We're still in this fight," he said in amazement.

"Yes. I don't know what you said to those creatures down there on that planet, but they came to this fight. And we would not still be alive had they not."

"Yeah, I went down there. I spoke to them. I pleaded with them to join us. They said no. They said they would not join this war, and that we could not stay here any longer."

Moye simply held out his hand, as if for Taylor to observe their presence.

"Sometimes we say one thing and do another," he added.

Taylor noted several of their allies' ships had been utterly destroyed, but he turned his attention to the Fatihi. Beam weapons and railguns were tearing the hull apart, and yet it still stood in defiance and kept firing.

One of the crew turned to the Captain and said something that was clearly important. Taylor turned to Moye for translation.

"We're getting a transmission from the Fatihi on an open channel."

The guns stopped firing on both sides while they waited for the impending negotiation.

"This should be good," he replied.

The Captain ordered the channel to be opened, and Erdogan stood on the bridge of the Fatihi. Taylor was expecting to be addressed personally at any moment, but he knew the creature couldn't know where he was, or even if he was alive.

"I am Lord Erdogan of the Krycenaean people. We came here to avenge the deaths of my family, and to end the scourge of the human race, who stand only to return and offend us if we leave them out here to revel in their failure and burning hatred of us."

Taylor couldn't believe his ears. He had never heard the enemy Lord speak like this, and he did not believe any of it.

"This is bullshit. It's all an act," he stated.

"Yes, and a convincing one. If he can convince our allies to leave us, we are finished."

Erdogan continued.

"Leave the humans to us, and we shall leave this system never to return. We only want what we came here for."

Taylor could see they were on very dangerous ground now, and there was nothing he could do. There was nobody he could negotiate with, nobody he could influence any further. Nor could he see the faces of their allies and get an inkling of their thoughts. All he could do was look out at the display screens for any sign of movement from their allies' vessels.

There was utter silence on the bridge, and Erdogan stood silently on the screen, awaiting a response.

Come on, stay with us, Taylor thought, over and over.

Finally, they saw one of the sleep alien vessels begin to light up, and a beam burst from its bow. It struck the Fatihi.

Erdogan staggered on screen before the transmission feed was lost. The bridge crew of the Diderot gave out a riotous cheer, as the rest of the fleet joined in the battle once again.

The firing went on for less than a minute when they saw the Fatihi open up a jump Gateway to escape. The human fleet and their allies continued relentlessly to hit the enemy's capitol ship and all who stood with her, but it wasn't enough. The Krys vessels were still firing as they fled. Just a few minutes later, the fleet was through the Gateway. It shut behind them, leaving the system in an eerie peace, where floating hulks served as coffins to the tens of thousands of dead on both sides. The crew of the Diderot looked at each other speechless and amazed to even be alive.

"Whatever you did, Colonel, you just saved us all," said Moye.

"I'm not sure I had a lot to do with it at all, Major, but I'll take the victory, pyrrhic or otherwise."

"Look at those ships. With those on side, we could win this war."

"Nobody said they are on our side yet," added Taylor, "They fought an invasion of their home system, is all."

"We've got an open transmission coming through from our alien friends," said Moye, relaying the message to Taylor.

The transmission opened, and the alien before them

looked just like Irala, but Taylor had no idea of who it actually was.

"You may land on our world, and we will do all we can to help with repairs. We have all lost greatly here today. Let us mourn our fallen."

The transmission ended there.

"Well that was...abrupt," added Moye.

"They aren't the most talkative of people, from what I can see. Took me forever just to get a name out of the one I met with."

"And the last time you spoke to them, they said leave this place, and that they would not fight. They just saved us and are inviting us down there. I think this war just took a turn the likes none of us could ever have imagined."

"I hope so," Taylor said with a sigh.

He was finding it hard to believe they might actually have a chance against Erdogan. He had long accepted they were fighting a losing battle, and he didn't want to get his hopes up, without the facts to support them. Admiral Huang appeared on a display. He had blood trickling down his face, and he held a bandage against the wound.

"Last reports were that Admiral Huber went down with his ship. Until we know otherwise, I am assuming command of the fleet. I am ordering all damaged vessels of the fleet to put down on the alien world to carry out repairs."

He looked down and appeared to be reaching for

some controls to end the transmission. It seemed he was having to do the job of several of his crew himself. The Captain of the Diderot turned to Taylor as if to ask for his approval, but Taylor said nothing.

"Are we to follow Huang now?" he asked.

"He was placed in second command of the fleet, so it seems appropriate to me, and he's speaking sense so far."

The Captain nodded and got up to approach Taylor. He held out his hand in friendship, and Taylor took it.

"I am Captain Lasure, and I am forever in your debt, Colonel."

"Do you have any news on survivors of the Washington?" he asked in return.

"The order to abandon ship was given in good time, and plenty managed to escape, though I have no idea on actual numbers."

"You think you can get us down onto that planet?"

"The ship is badly damaged, but she'll make it. She's kept us safe through the worst of it this so far."

Taylor nodded in agreement. He could see warning lights and diagrams all about on the screens of the bridge. He could tell there wasn't a lot still holding them together, and he would give anything to get his feet on firm ground once more. Moye stepped up to him.

"How did you know the door would kill that Juggernaut?"

"I didn't," he replied quickly, "but it was the only chance

we had."

Moye laughed.

"So you gambled it all on that hope of achieving something you had never tried before, and had no idea if it would work?"

"I wouldn't say it was much of a gamble, Major. It was either my plan working, or all of us dying."

Moye slapped his hand down on Taylor's shoulder in a friendly fashion.

"You really are crazy, Colonel, but perhaps just the right sought of crazy for this war."

He'd made a friend there, and he knew how valuable that was.

"I always thought you were an arrogant son of a bitch, but now I get it," added Moye, "Your way isn't my way, but I understand it. Were there a bar nearby, I'd happily buy you a drink."

"We'll sure find something."

But Taylor was distracted, thinking of his own unit and those he had fought beside for so many years. And Eli.

"How long until we reach the surface?" he asked Lasure.

"We are still conducting running repairs and limping her all the way. We are going to have to save much of our power for the descent into the atmosphere. Maybe we'll be there in an hour."

It felt like an age to wait, but that was all he could do now, when he suddenly thought about why he came aboard in the first place.

"Got to be Mechs still aboard, Moye, and we need to flush them out."

"Relax, Colonel, we already have our marines doing that very task."

Lasure turned back as he heard the comment.

"Yes, and you've shown yourself more than capable of defending the bridge. If it would be agreeable to you, Colonel, we'd all feel a lot safer if you watched over us until we reached the surface."

He agreed to do so, understanding the Captain was in fact suggesting he rested. He took a seat on the floor, propping himself against the wall near the blast door and waited. It felt like a long haul to reach the planet, and as they finally made their descent, he stood next to the Captain, looking at the display screens of the grounded fleet they were approaching. Most had made it before them, and it was a shattered fleet.

"It'll take us months to get these ships up and running again, if at all," said Lasure.

"Erdogan suffered at least as much as we did. I think we've bought ourselves more than enough time to prepare for the next move."

"Next move?" Moye asked, "Isn't this the sign that we're staying and making a life for ourselves here?"

"I don't know about any of you, but I won't settle down anywhere, knowing that bastard sits atop a throne over our world. I will not stop. I will not stop fighting and trying to get back home. Nothing will stop me but death."

"And if that's what you find?"

"Well, then better I died trying, Major, than lived in exile out here."

"Do you regret leaving Earth?"

He had to think about it for a few moments. It was something he'd thought about often and could still not make up his mind.

"Yes and no. I regret leaving so many of our own kind down there, and I can only pray they have somehow made it, although I don't see how. But how could we have ever won down there? Now with allies, we might stand some hope, but alone, we were defeated."

They could hear the ship's structure creaking under the strain of the entrance into the atmosphere, and it shook so violently Taylor wondered if they'd even make it to the surface alive.

"Never did much like flying."

"Then perhaps you should not have joined the marines."

"Well, we can't always get what we want."

The ship reached the surface and put down on an empty plain of desert with twenty-five other ships of the human fleet. Their alien allies were nowhere to be seen. As the landing ramp went down, Taylor was the first one striding down it and finally felt the earth beneath his feet. It was a relief.

"Taylor!" a voice cried.

He turned to see Parker running towards him. It was the most amazing feeling he had felt in weeks. The possibility of loss, and the realisation she was still alive, was overwhelming. She leapt into his arms, and he felt a surge of excitement overcome him.

"I've looked all over for you, every ship down here. I just kept looking and looking. I knew you couldn't be dead."

"I saw the Washington go down and my heart sank," he replied.

"They just came out of nowhere and kept hitting us. Didn't even have much chance to fight back. Before we knew it, the Admiral was ordering an evacuation."

"And what of the Admiral?"

"He went down with the ship. He stayed there until the end to man the targeting systems and keep the guns firing. He wouldn't let anyone else stay with him."

"His loss will be felt, but none of us could have asked any more of him. And our people?"

"Scattered throughout a number of ships. Jafar is with King, looking for you as well. Morris is wounded, but he should be okay. At least half of our unit has made it. Still waiting on contact from any others. It's a complete mess down here, right now. Come on, I'll take you to King. He has been in charge until now. Last time I saw him, he was hounding Admiral Huang to send out search parties for you."

"I bet that went down well."

She took his arm and hauled him forwards. They weaved their way between hordes of personnel, many being attended by medics or their own comrades. They reached a temporary command structure and could see King stepping out with his shoulders slumped and looking thoroughly demoralised. Jafar stood waiting to address him.

"Captain King!" Taylor hollered.

King looked up in amazement, his eyes suddenly lit up, and Jafar followed close beside him.

"How? Where the hell were you?"

"Made it on to the Diderot and did what I could there."

It was all they needed to hear, but before they could exchange any more pleasantries, Taylor heard his name being called. He turned and found Irala standing there. Just as before, he seemed to appear out of nowhere.

"You fought with us," stated Taylor, "Thank you. Had you not, we would surely have been defeated."

"My people had long sought to forget Erdogan and the wounds he had inflicted on us. But we could hold ourselves back no longer. The wounds cut deep, and seeing your people suffer at his hands was enough to remind us of the fact."

"So you're with us?" Taylor asked.

Irala avoided the question and instead turned to Jafar.

"Still you trust this one at your side? He is one of them? Worse still, one of the personal aides to a Krycenaean Lord."

"I know."

"And you know it was ones just like him that have laid waste to your homes, and did so to ours?"

"Ones like him yes, but not him. There are evildoers in all races, all nations, and all peoples, but I do not believe any of us are born that way. Jafar has more than proven himself to me, and I would trust him with my life, and I will not accept you treating him any differently to myself."

Irala nodded and seemed to accept the situation.

"Follow me," he stated.

He led Taylor through the crowds and vessels out into the open plain until they were long out of hearing distance of anyone.

"My people have agreed to allow you to live here. I believe we can live together peacefully."

Taylor shook his head.

"This is not agreeable to you?"

"You saw what Erdogan just did. He'll be back when he has recovered, and he'll be back in far greater number. He won't stop coming."

"What would you do?"

"Take the fight to him. We know he'll be on Earth. It's the paradise they fought so hard to reach. We take the fight to him, kill him, and retake my world, where you can then live also."

Irala thought about it for some time.

"If we do this, the price will be great. Far greater than you can believe."

"I understand loss, and I am willing to accept it."

"I do not think you have experienced this kind of loss before."

"What, can you see the future now?"

"No, but we calculate and investigate with precise knowledge and mathematics. We predict the future with science."

"Well, if you'd tried to calculate my chances of getting this far, you'd probably have me dead years ago."

"It is only fair to warn you. You will lose more than I believe you can afford."

"If that is the price of victory, I will gladly pay it."

"And what is victory to you?"

"Total victory. Erdogan dead. His armies defeated, whether they surrender or die. Our world back."

"Total victory?" Irala asked.

He seemed to go blank as if he were communicating with others through some strange means. Taylor still wondered what his role within their society was, but it didn't matter in that moment.

"Then we are agreed. We will fight together, until total victory."

Taylor smiled and held out his hand. The alien took it

as if highly familiar with the human gesture.

"Welcome to the cause," Taylor added gleefully.

CHAPTER FIVE

"Everyone ready?" Kelly asked.

He got a series of acknowledgements, and then looked to Becker and the last of his tank crews; they were assembled at a bank of remote access computers in the back of a box truck.

"Think this will work?" Becker asked.

"Those bastards are pretty simple. They target the biggest most powerful target and destroy it before moving down the line. We show them enough force, and they'll buy it.

"Five tanks?"

"It's a bigger threat than the rest of us pose, right now."

"On my mark, five, four, three, two, one, go, go, go!"

The hidden bunker door in the hangar bay slid open and creaked, pulling foliage back with it. It was the first and last time it would ever do so since they arrived. The five main battle tanks rolled forward out through the opening and split off into two detachments. They headed in opposing directions to flank around the base and towards the enemy's original landing point. As they finally disappeared from view, Kelly gave the second order.

"Move out!"

The sounds of the megaphone on the vehicle echoed around the hangar bay for all to hear; their radios were jammed just as they always were by their alien enemy. Fifty vehicles, mostly soft skinned, rushed forward for the opening.

"You know this is a crazy plan, right?"

"Of course it is, Becker. The fact we are still alive to do it is crazy, so what do you expect?" he responded.

Kelly watched from his screen as they made their way out onto a narrow track that led through the thick undergrowth and had complete cover due to the forest canopy. They had two armoured trucks out ahead of them to lead the convoy, and they were the third in line. He was content that they were on track and went over and stood over Becker's shoulder, watching the Captain control one of the tanks as if it were a video game.

"No gunner, no loader, no driver," he complained.

"Just do the best you can do," Kelly murmured.

The five of them were the only remaining tank crew at Becker's disposal, and therefore each had to control a vehicle.

"We can only go on as long as those magazines load. Once they're out or jammed, we're fucked."

"Don't worry about that. You just cause as much trouble as you possibly can. The aim is to stop them coming after us for as long as possible."

"And if they ignore out armour altogether, and just come right for us?"

"Well, we'll cross that bridge, if we come to it."

"That is reassuring."

"I thought so."

They carried on in silence, and Kelly watched Becker's screen. The tank crashed through undergrowth. Becker had a semi circular display that gave him great visibility in front and to the side of the vehicle. It almost made him feel as if in his commander's seat, but at the same time, thankful not to be. As the vehicle forced its way through one large piece of foliage, they were suddenly met with the view of an enemy aircraft on the ground. An opening had been created from the shell bursts destroying so many trees in the battle for the bunker. A number of Mechs were unloading from what appeared to be a small transport.

"Hello," said Becker in an unnerving voice.

He clicked a trigger on the joystick in his right hand. The screen lit up, and the gun barrel flashed. The shell hit the aircraft dead on. It pierced right through the flank and ignited, blowing the vehicle apart.

"Woohoo!" Becker shouted.

The Mech survivors scattered as he took aim a second time. The main gun had reloaded in just three seconds. He fired once again, and the high explosive shell struck two Mechs and blew them apart with no effort at all. Next he panned the gun over to another Mech that was firing back at them. The pulses were striking the tank, doing little if anything at all. He fired again, and the creature vanished in a ball of fire.

"Starting to like this!"

"Yeah, well don't get too used to it. All good things must come to an end."

"But it's so much fun," Becker joked, pulling the trigger once again.

Kelly turned back to their vehicle display screen that looked ahead. There was still no sign of trouble. He looked down at the scanners; they weren't picking up anything in the air either.

"Think we've made it?" Engel asked.

She was sitting at the screens nearby, keeping an eye out as he went from one to another.

"Too soon to say, but they reckoned on a siege, and probably aren't all that ready for a chase. I figure we've got a solid chance."

He watched the tankers display screens. One of them suddenly went blank, and the operator hit the controls and swore at the screen. Kelly rested his hands on the man's shoulders.

"Relax, that's what you were there to do. We always knew they'd fall. That's why you're driving them from in here."

He turned around to see two Juggernauts running towards the screen of another, which was an unsettling sight. The gun fired. It hit one head on, and it exploded. But the gun could not reload fast enough. The other Juggernaut reached the tank and leapt atop it like a wild animal. It was out of view now, and they could only see the screen shaking while it tried to take the vehicle apart. The operator did the only thing he could; ignore it entirely. The gun fired again, and they could see at least one Mech blown apart by the shell.

The legs of the Juggernaut came into view now, and it seemed to be kicking down on the barrel of the gun, trying to break it with sheer strength. Finally, the barrel buckled slightly, and the operator smiled as he pulled the trigger. They saw a massive blast ignite, just as the camera went to black. They could only imagine what had happened to the enemy beside it.

"We've got contact up ahead, Sir," said Engel.

Kelly turned and saw a group of Mechs landing in a small clearing ahead. One of their vehicles had already opened fire.

"Keep at it," he said, climbing a ladder onto the roof. He took up position in a small, enclosed machine gun turret on top of the command vehicle. It was equipped with two linked up heavy machine guns, and Kelly was itching to put them to use. He took aim at the craft first and let rip with a vicious burst of gunfire. It riddled the hull with holes. The craft tried to gain altitude and escape, but he tracked it and kept the trigger held down. It was engulfed in flames and crashed down into undergrowth. He quickly turned the weapon on the Mechs below, who weren't prepared for the storm coming their way. One of the vehicles ahead hit one with the corner of its reinforced bumper and smashed it out the way. Kelly panned the gun around and kept firing. They passed the remaining creatures and watched as the vehicles behind them finished them off, without slowing at all.

Kelly climbed back down to check on Becker's crews. Only the Captain and one other were still in the fight. The others watched the two remaining screens and egged on their friends. Becker's screen showed a few dozen Mechs lying dead or dying, but he was still driving forward and heading right for the survivors. As he did so, one of the Juggernauts appeared from a bunker wall and stood in defiance; ready to charge at him like a raging bull.

"Okay, you bastard, have a taste of this," he said, taking aim and pulling the trigger. The shell hit the creature dead on, and it disappeared as the high explosive shell ignited.

That at least brought a smile to Kelly's face.

"They're all over me!" the other operator screamed. Becker looked around to his screen. The Mechs swamping the vehicle were placing charges, and a Juggernaut tried to tear open the hatch on top of the turret. The tracks had already been knocked off it, and it was clear the vehicle was about to be destroyed. Becker turned his own turret around and took aim at the lower right where he knew the main ammo rack store was. He took careful aim and pulled the trigger.

The shell went right through into the rack. An almighty explosion obliterated all the enemy surrounding the vehicle. Becker took a deep breath and sighed.

"It was all I could do."

He pivoted his turret around to look for a new target. He could see an enemy aircraft come in low to a hover position and fire a large pulse weapon. It struck the flank of his own tank, and his screen instantly went blank. They had no idea if the vehicle was destroyed or just the remote equipment damaged, but the result was the same.

"Well that's it then," stated Becker, "That's all the armour we had, and probably all we'll ever have again."

"It did its job," replied Kelly, "All this equipment we have. All it is here for is to provide for our safety. Good work all of you. You raised hell, certainly."

"That's what we were training for. But without our tanks, we might as well be civilians," replied Becker.

"No such thing anymore. You're either a fighter or you're dead."

They were all silent, waiting for his next command.

"That aircraft that took you out, I'm guessing it'll be coming for us soon enough. Hopefully, they haven't got many more. Everything they were gearing up for was for a ground assault. We just changed the environment, and with any luck, it'll take time for them to adapt. Priority right now is making a clean break, and we can't do that while they have anything in the air nearby that is tracking us."

"What do you suggest?"

"Becker, my guess is anything they have in the air will be coming right for us, trying to do some damage rather than keep an eye on our location. We can use that. We draw them in and knock them out of the sky all at once."

"Draw them in?" asked Engel, "Haven't we had enough to deal with, without bringing in more trouble?"

Kelly took in a deep breath.

"I know exactly how you feel. But if they track us for much longer, we'll never escape. I doubt they have more than a handful of vehicles up there right now, and they'll all be looking for us. I reckon we have a couple of hours at best before they bring in some serious hardware, and then we've got no chance at all."

"How do you want to play this, then?" Becker asked.

He looked at a map displayed on one of the screens.

"The lead vehicles already know what I have in mind. They're taking us here," he said, pointing to an opening in the base of a valley.

"Looks like a killing field, for them."

"Yep, and I'm hoping that's just how they feel about it. We make it look as if we're stopping there to rest up and devise our next strategy."

"You think they'll fall for that?"

"It's a big juicy target. I can't see how they couldn't."

"And if they fall for it so bad that they come down on us like a tonne of bricks?"

"As I said, I don't believe they have a lot more to throw at us, here and now. We reel them in, and take them down in one."

Becker nodded. "Better than anything else I can think of."

"Good. I've had anti-aircraft weapons installed on five of the larger vehicles in the convoy. A number of others have turrets with heavy machine guns that are easily capable of doing damage at anything that flies low and slow enough."

"And will they, Sir?"

"What, Engel?"

"Fly low and slow enough?"

"They'll have to. It's a steep sided valley. It'll make it difficult to approach for strafing runs, and we haven't seen anything resembling any kind of bomber. They'll have to come into the valley and hover to enable them to drop troops and target us effectively."

"Sounds like you've got it all worked out," said Becker.

"You didn't think I'd come out here without a plan, did you?" he replied with a smile.

"And there's me thinking we just ran for the hills."

"We made it this far partly through luck, but more through strategy and the ability of our troops," he added, "Don't ever forget that."

Ten minutes later, they were at the opening, exactly as Kelly had said. It looked like a perfect ambush spot had the enemy known they'd be there. As they rolled into the exposed valley, they half expected to drive into such an ambush, but nothing came. They rocked up into position as planned. Kelly climbed up onto the roof of the command vehicle so he could see and control everything from the point of observation. He could see the crews of the larger trucks pulling back the canopies, revealing the multi barrelled anti-aircraft guns, like he'd used when they were attacked in their hometown.

He turned around slowly and studied the hundreds of soldiers still at his command. None of them sat about skulking and waiting to die. They did not complain or show any inkling of wanting to give up. They all set about their jobs to ready themselves for the next fight. It took barely three minutes after the vehicles had come to a standstill, to having everyone prepared for the battle. Only Becker's tank crews looked lost now. They had rifles in hand but didn't seem to know what to do.

"Becker, your people are to guard this truck. Engel,

you're staying close to those scanners at all times and relaying every piece of information you get to me."

Everyone had settled down into their positions and looked to him for something, but he wasn't sure he had anything to give them.

"All those alien bastards that enter this valley to get us must die. You will not show mercy. You will not let any escape. Our continued survival depends on us putting some distance on them! So when they come down into this valley, you wait until they're as close as they can be till you shoot. You do not risk a single one of them escaping, you hear me!"

There were groans and grunts of approval. He knew it was much to ask them to kill the enemy; only for them to hold their fire long enough to reel them in.

"Nobody fires until I give the command!"

They were silent now. Confident and ready to do what needed to be done.

"Should this fail. If the enemy overrun us, and you are forced to flee, then do so. Split up, and try and make it your own way. We don't set any rendezvous point. If you are divided, then I wish you luck; I wish us all luck!"

He couldn't think of anything else to say, so simply sat down on the rooftop by the turret and waited for some word from Engel. He took the time to carefully observe their location, phasing out all that was manmade that they had taken there. He took in the beauty of the location and the sweet clean air. He knew it wouldn't last for much longer, so he cherished it while he could. For all that he hated the Krys for forcing him off of his home colony, he truly appreciated moments like this. They were a natural bliss he never experienced in the environmentally controlled confinements of their accommodation on the Moon.

Finally, the word came in, "Sir, I've got three targets incoming!"

He sighed; knowing the beauty around him was about to be so rudely interrupted.

"Okay, people, remember what you have to do!"

He climbed into the turret on the rooftop and waited for the enemy to come into view.

Wait, wait! Come on, you bastards, he told himself.

He was looking forward to seeing the enemy now. They had forced him from his home once again, and he wanted blood for it.

"They're almost on top of us, Sir!"

"Good, you keep that information coming," he replied.

Then he saw the first of them. It was nothing more than a silhouette at first. It came over the trees at the top of the valley and then dived in towards them. He waited and waited, resisting the urge to fire, despite tracking his target all the way. Another two small ships followed it. He took a deep breath and slowed his breathing to keep calm. He saw the flash of a gun on the lead ship, and the pulse struck the ground not far from his vehicle. But still he did not fire. A few more pulses struck the ground.

Finally, he saw the nose light on the lead craft as it slowed its descent to come to a hover position. He didn't have to give the command; his trigger finger did it for him. The two machine guns in front of him roared to life, and a burst of fire smashed into the nose of the aircraft before him. Just as the first impacts struck, he saw another five enemy aircraft enter the valley. The timing was perfect.

The closest ship he had hit was struck by a hail of fire from the rapid firing anti-aircraft platforms all around him. The two craft with it tried to bank and gain speed, but it was too late for them also. They burst into flames and dropped out of the sky. A few Mechs managed to jump from one, and Kelly's troops on the ground were quick to take aim and finish them as they landed.

Kelly turned his gun on the next targets. They had split on entering the valley and seen the incoming fire, to spread out. They were already raining in fire against the troops below. A pulse flattened one of the smaller trucks and its two crew sheltering beside it. Kelly squeezed the trigger once again and riddled one of the craft with fire. It began disembarking Mechs in an assisted fifty-metre drop with boosters. His machine gun followed them down and cut two of them apart before they'd even reached the canyon floor.

Anti-aircraft fire filled the sky, in what could almost

be described as a fireworks display. The soldiers on the ground cheered as each of the craft was brought down with ruthless efficiency. They were all nothing more than light transports that didn't stand a chance against close range heavy weapons fire.

A number of the Mechs had managed to disembark from one of the craft before it was destroyed and had got under the anti-aircraft firing solutions. They were out from cover now and striding towards one of the AA trucks. Kelly rotated his gun around and took aim at the first. He opened fire and blew it apart, but he could see a pulse from one of the others coming right for the armoured canopy of his emplacement. He ducked down barely in time; the pulse impacted and blew the canopy, showering shards of reinforced Perspex down on him. Several of them burnt into the flesh on his face and neck, but a few seconds later, he was back up at the guns that were now open to the world.

Kelly fired once again, this time keeping his finger on the trigger as he strafed three of the Mechs. With the weight of fire from others, they were rapidly brought down. He quickly turned his attention back to the air. Another of the craft dropped from the sky and barrelled into nearby trees and burst into flames. But he turned his attention now to the final craft and could see it was banking and putting full power down to escape the valley.

"Bring it down!"

His voice echoed around the valley through the loudhailer on his vehicle for all to hear. He opened fire with his own guns but was out of ammo after the initial burst. He knew there was no chance of reloading in time now and simply watched, hoping his people could do it. Tracer fire lit up the sky as the alien craft tried evasive manoeuvres. It was almost out of view when a final burst struck the engines, and it lost altitude, clipping the trees at the top of the valley and crashing down the other side.

"Did they make it?" he asked Engel hastily.

"No...no, Sir."

He looked back. The smoke was rising from where the craft had gone down, and he sighed in relief.

"We did it," he told himself.

He looked all around them for some sign of remaining Mechs and heard a few shots as the last two were gunned down. As he climbed up onto the top of the vehicle, he could see four of their own vehicles had been destroyed by the blast, and he could see as many bodies or more. No losses were acceptable, but the result was the best they could hope for. He looked down the hatch of the turret towards the ladder leading into the vehicle and asked one last time.

"Any more contact?"

"No, Sir, the air is clear."

"Then we've done it."

He looked out to the rest of his people who waited

their next orders.

"You make me proud!" he said sternly. A single tear dropped down his face and seeped into the burning wound on his cheek, "You've just won us another day, another week, another month. It doesn't matter how long. We're still alive. We're still fighting. We are the resistance!"

Cheers rang out, but he knew he couldn't revel in it for too long. He held up his hand to call for silence. Almost instantly the valley returned to the tranquillity he had enjoyed in the moments before the battle.

"We may be on the run, but we have achieved exactly what we set out to achieve!"

More cheers followed, and once again he had to call for silence.

"The fact remains that we are still here. We live on in defiance, and every single day that one of us still breathes and fights, is another day we have succeeded in our mission!"

There were nods and grunts of approval, but they stayed silent this time for him to continue.

"So we go on. We run when we have to and fight where we can. We've just bought ourselves the time we need to blend back into this vast forest, but we cannot linger any longer. Gather up the wounded. Leave the dead, or risk joining them. Let's move out!"

Nobody liked leaving their fallen friends where they fell, but nobody argued the point. They all knew they couldn't afford to. It took less than a minute for everyone to clamber into the vehicles. Kelly's was already rocking forward in less time than that. He climbed down into the comms cab and found Engel waiting for him. She was staring at him. He froze for a moment and tried to figure out what she wanted from him.

"You did well," he finally stated.

"All I did was sit here and tell you what I saw."

"We all have a job to do, none of them are glamorous, but all of them are necessary."

"I want to fight."

"Why?" he asked abruptly, "You weren't trained for it."

"I wasn't trained for anything that is required of any of us anymore. There are plenty of civilians around who weren't trained as soldiers either."

"If this is about doing your part, then trust me, you are already doing it."

She looked away and to her instruments, knowing she wasn't getting anywhere. He paced over to her and put his hand on her chin, turning her head around to face him.

"Trust me, your time to fight with a rifle in hand will come. It will come for all of us. That doesn't mean you'd wish it to come sooner rather than later."

"But...you like to fight," she pleaded.

He shook his head. "What gave you that impression?"

"All the speeches you give. It's like all you want in life is to kill the enemy."

"But not because I enjoy it. Anyone who ever tells you they do is either a fool or crazy. It brings me great satisfaction knowing we have deprived the enemy of something, but I get no pleasure from the killing."

He knew deep down that he was lying to some extent, but he wanted to believe he was better than that. He also knew he had to set an example.

What would Taylor do? he asked himself.

He was certain his answer would be the same as his.

Try and set a higher standard than that which I live by.

Kelly turned his attention to Becker who also looked a little lost.

"You all right, Captain?"

He shrugged. "I'm still alive."

"Then what's the problem?"

"I'm a tanker with no tanks left. Leaves me, well, useless."

Kelly laughed.

"We win this victory, and in large part at your hands, and you sulk about it. Don't you worry, we'll find plenty for you to do."

With that, he climbed back up the ladder and into the damaged turret to use as an observation post. He watched the column fall into line, and they moved back under the canopy of the forest. He had no idea where they were heading, only that it was away from the enemy, and that was enough.

* * *

Just six days had passed, and Kelly sat around a campfire with Reynolds and Becker. He knew depression was setting in amongst the ranks. They still had food to last plenty of time, but the temporary shelters and lack of security of the bunker made them all uneasy. A canopy above them kept them dry as the rain poured onto the ground everywhere around them. He watched Engel climbed out of the command vehicle where she'd been sleeping in the back with several others. Few of them got more than an hour or two's sleep each night. They were being hunted, and they knew it. It was that feeling alone that kept them awake at night.

"Is this the glorious guerrilla warfare you had in mind?" Becker asked. He was wearing every item of clothing he owned to stay warm, "It'll be snowing any day now," he added.

"Well, you're a cheery one, aren't you?" Kelly answered him.

"Only saying what I see."

"You don't see snow though, do you? Why pre-empt problems?"

Becker shrugged his shoulders.

"If it snows, it snows. If it rains, it rains. And if a hundred Mechs turn up tonight to blow your head off, then so be it. Maybe that'll happen, but there's nothing you can do about that either," Kelly spat.

Even as he finished the sentence, he regretted having said it. He opened his mouth to speak again but stopped, knowing anything he said would probably make things worse.

"You know we aren't the first people to fight out in this wilderness. These lands have a long history of harbouring armies that have beaten those of far greater odds, or at least provided the safety and security to those here to live long enough for others to come to their aid," said Engel.

"But there isn't anyone, is there?" asked Reynolds.

"Anyone where?" Engel asked.

"Coming to our aid. Nobody coming to break the siege or haul us out of here."

Kelly shook his head.

"You're as bad as Becker. He wants to think we're already finished, and you want to rule out all hope of there being other survivors."

"You think there are?"

"Of course," Kelly replied abruptly, "You think we're the only ones capable of holding out this long? What we have achieved is impressive, I would say, but don't underestimate the rest of the world."

"Pockets of survivors like us maybe, but not enough to ever come to our aid. Can you imagine us being able to ride to the aid of others?"

"Well, Becker, maybe we should. Maybe that would give us something to go on for, beyond just revenge.

"And survival," added Reynolds.

"I'd rather have died in the seat of my tank than live like a wild animal out here until I'm finally hunted down and put to death. I'm not sure this is survival but anymore than a prolonged agonising death."

Kelly looked at Becker in disgust. He pointed out towards the rest of their people camped all around. "You know they rely on us to keep it together. That means they depend on you, so start acting like the officer you are."

They all fell silent and thought on his words. Kelly knew they were heading for disaster. They needed either hope or a battle to fight. He prayed there was someone coming to their aid one day. It seemed a dream beyond any logic or sense, but he could still hope.

CHAPTER SIX

Taylor stood on top of the Diderot, watching the world go by. Ever since his time aboard the ship, he had felt an attachment to it. On an alien world where he had no home, and the Washington was long gone, it seemed the only place he had a connection with. In the distance was line after line of temporary structures, assembled to house the personnel without accommodation on the vessels that had either been destroyed or were being repaired and refitted. Jafar was standing just a few metres behind him and was, as he always preferred, glued to his side.

"You know it's a goddamn miracle they haven't tried to kill you yet," Taylor said to him.

"Not really," he replied casually.

Taylor turned, somewhat surprised.

"They gave you their word, and you gave them yours. I have nothing to fear."

"And you trust that whole heartedly?"

"I have no reason not to. They could have killed me any time they liked. Were they still intending to, there would be nothing to stop them."

"So don't worry about what you can't change?"

Jafar shrugged as if to agree in part.

"Look at these ships," said Taylor, "We're scraping bits together to try and get them operational. At least half of them should never be committed to space again. They'll be damn death traps. We need the tech they have."

"Who?"

"Irala's people, whoever they are. How do we not even know what they're called yet? You know we are goddamn allies, and I've not heard a word from them. Sure, they must be repairing and recovering themselves, but not a single bit of contact? Time we got some contact from them."

Jafar didn't respond, but Taylor knew his silence was a statement in itself.

"What, you don't agree?"

"If they have not come to you, they may not want to talk."

"And if we don't go to them, how will we ever know? I'm gonna go find that silent son of a bitch and get some answers."

Taylor intended to leave but was suddenly met with Irala standing in front of him. He jumped back a few paces in surprise.

"How the hell do you do that?"

"You have encountered Erdogan enough times now to know that he possesses hologram projection technology?"

"Yeah."

"He stole that from us. One of many devices he stole in the war we fought."

Taylor thought himself a fool for not reaching that conclusion, but he still found it hard to adjust to the ever-increasing amount of tech he encountered.

"That cloaking technology I have seen your ships use. I have seen it before."

"Yes, though his people were never able to make it work effectively for larger vessels, and only ever in a limited number of equipment taken from us."

"If you possessed such technology, how did you ever lose?" Taylor asked.

"We are few, we always have been. We live for hundreds; sometimes even thousands of your years, but we have few offspring and are a small people in population. Hence, we rely on our technology to make up for this."

"If you live that long, then dying must be a pretty big deal?"

"Individually, no more a loss than I should imagine you would feel, but as a species, yes."

"Well, we're starting to understand that. We aren't exactly a flourishing population. There are what, three million humans left? We've entered a new dark age."

Irala looked surprised by his comment.

"There are many more than three million of you left."

"What do you mean?"

"Those on Earth, of course, your homeworld."

"Earth is long lost, and Erdogan would not have let humanity survive in his paradise."

Irala shook his head. "Then you are misinformed. Pockets of resistance fight on in your world. Others have been enslaved and work for the Krys."

Taylor was shocked and speechless. He had never believed life could have gone on in any capacity after they left.

"How do you know this?"

"We have monitored the progression of the war on your planet."

"So you have people there now?"

"No."

"Do you know how many humans still live?"

"Our last figures suggest up to eighty or ninety million worldwide."

Taylor was once again silenced and shocked.

"I need to pass this information on to our leaders. I don't think you appreciate how significant this is."

Irala didn't respond physically; he only calmly responded, "You will in time tell them."

"They'll need to meet you. I do not command this fleet,

far from it."

"But we have dealt with you, we trust you. We do not know them, and we do not know whether we trust them yet."

"Well, you won't know till you meet them, will you?"

"For now, we will make all contact through you, Colonel. You have proven yourself to my people. Though we can still not approve of your association with that," he said as he pointed to Jafar, "You should have killed it the first time you set eyes upon it. For that creature can bring you nothing but pain and destruction."

"And if I had killed him all those years ago, I wouldn't be here to talk to you this day. You expect a lot of trust from me, so I expect a little back. When we finally take Earth back, we'll have a sizeable Krys population to deal with, and I won't have them exterminated as one of their leaders once tried with us. Jafar shows there is a way we can live together."

Taylor couldn't believe he was saying it but realised it is what they needed.

Irala seemed wholly unconvinced, but he moved past the issue.

"You say you want to go back to your Earth and fight Erdogan there, but your ships look far from ready."

Taylor smiled in response.

"If we were on our world, at our shipyards with our resources and workers, we might get these ships up and running and ready to go. But we're not. We're on a foreign world, with no shipyards, and nothing more than what we brought with us. We could sure do with the help of the locals."

Irala was still silent.

"What'll it be?" Taylor asked, "We're allies now. Will you help us be the best we can be so that together we stand a chance?"

"What you are asking us is to share our technology with you?"

Taylor nodded.

"We do not yet know whether you present a threat to us or not."

"And yet you fight with us?"

"We have a shared enemy, that does not mean we present no threat to each other."

Taylor sighed. "We have a chance together, but not if we stand as allies of convenience. We have to be more than that, or we don't stand a chance at all. The fight we had with Erdogan, we fought to a stalemate with everything we had. If we are gonna take him on at Earth, well… that's his home soil now. He's got everything going for him. We couldn't beat him when we had the world's armies at our disposal, so how can we have any hope of success now?"

"You wanted this," replied Irala.

"Yes, I wanted to fight back the best way we can. With a little help from you, we could be stronger fighters. We

126

could have better weapons, better ships. We could stand a real chance. Why will you not help us?"

"You ask a lot of us."

"Yes I do, and I offer a lot more if we succeed together. You've seen our world. Tell me it isn't an improvement over this piece of shit desert? Tell me it isn't what your people deserve?"

"I will discuss it with my people. I will meet you here at noon tomorrow."

"On whose clock?"

"According to what your watch is set to."

Taylor looked at his watch and nodded in agreement. He looked back and opened his mouth to ask another question, but Irala was gone.

"Why does he always have to do that?"

He looked around to Jafar but got no response.

"He doesn't like you, you realise that right?" Taylor asked him.

"Neither did you when we first met. You tried to kill me, too."

"Fair point."

The time until their meeting seemed to pass quickly as he watched Parker and the other NCOs continue training new recruits from the civilians who had volunteered. As noon approached on that second day, he waited aboard the roof of the Diderot with Admiral Huang and five other high-ranking officers. It was a bizarre location to have such an official and unprecedented gathering, but Taylor rather appreciated it. They could see for miles all around, and yet had relative privacy from those below. Jafar stood a few metres behind them, too, Captain King with him, as well as several marines working as a protection detail for Admiral Huang.

Taylor still wasn't sure what he thought of the Chinaman, but at least he appeared a strong and decisive leader, and that meant a lot.

"Where are they, Colonel?" Huang asked.

Taylor looked down at his watch. It was one minute to noon, and he was counting the seconds down. He looked up as they hit the hour, and three of the aliens appeared before him.

"I am Admiral Huang of the human fleet."

"Irala, of the Aranui."

Taylor was surprised.

At last, now we know what to call them.

Huang was shocked at the sight of the Aranui and wasn't sure how to proceed. Taylor stepped in and opened the conversation even though he knew it was far above his station.

"We're here to discuss your assistance," he stated, "We need materials, and we need your technologies and knowledge to make us the best we can be."

Huang glanced at him, clearly irritated but finally nodded in agreement and looked back to Irala to await a response.

"We have considered your request," replied Irala.

There was a long silence, and they waited for him to continue.

"We have misplaced our trust in other beings in the past and paid a dear price for it. Therefore, we will assist you, but only as far as we choose, and within strict parameters."

"Anything you can do would be greatly appreciated," Huang said quietly.

"The first requirement is that we deal with those we trust. At this time, that is only Colonel Taylor."

"He is a fine marine, but he is not a representative of our fleet or our race."

Irala went silent and stared Huang down until he changed his mind. It was clear he would accept nothing else.

"That is what we will do. What will you do, Colonel?"

"Seems to me we need to do two things. We need to organise an invasion force, and to begin smaller scale attacks that weaken Erdogan's forces before we are ready for the former."

Huang didn't look impressed that Taylor was calling the shots, but he knew he was powerless to affect it. Taylor carried on.

"I believe if we can draw Erdogan out and kill him, the ground operation will be comparatively easy. When Demiran fell, his armies lay down arms for the most part.

More than anything, I want to reach out and put some hurt on him, make him bleed. Make him and his armies know that we can make them bleed on what is now their home soil. Let them know how that feels."

"If we are to carry out operations in your solar system, then there is an obstacle we must overcome. A new defence grid they have assembled stops us from carrying out many potential operations on the surface."

"Perfect, then we hit that first," said Taylor excitedly.

It was like a dream come true that he never could have imagined possible.

"Everything was going so quickly that Huang could not get a word in, and Taylor stepped past him now to bypass the Admiral entirely.

"Give us the means, and we'll nail that fucking station," said Taylor.

"You'll need Jump technology to do it. We'll install six of your vessels with such technology, but no more. With a combined fleet, we will strike the defence grid platform in seven days."

"Seven days?" Huang interrupted, "We have only just begun repairs on our vessels and not even buried all our dead yet. We aren't ready to be striking back, not by a long shot."

Irala ignored him and looked to Taylor.

"We can prepare your ships. Are you ready for it?" he asked, "You are asking us to make a leap of faith, as you call it. We ask that you prove you are willing to give as much as you ask for."

"Give us the opportunity to strike at Erdogan, and I will give you everything I have got, and more," replied Taylor.

"Then select six of your medium-sized vessels that can carry fighters and a sizeable contingent of your soldiers."

"Marines," replied Taylor.

"You travel in space aboard ships than never encounter water, and yet still you call yourself a marine?"

"Some traditions are worth holding on to, no matter where life takes you."

Irala seemed impressed. "The finest answer. Select your vessels, and have them moved one kilometre south of this position. Have their flight crews and maintenance teams stay with them. We will outfit your vessels and have your crews familiarised with them within five days."

Huang opened his mouth to speak, but before he'd got a single syllable out, the three aliens had vanished.

"Colonel Taylor!" he yelled furiously.

Taylor turned to him casually.

"Have you forgotten who is in charge of this fleet?"

"Admiral, we're a pretty long way past any kind of protocol here. I don't know you, and I certainly never signed up to serve under you. In time, I might call you the boss, but right now, I've got a technologically advanced race willing to give me the means to hit back and to take back my home, and I'm gonna take it. Now you can either stand with me, and help take back our planet, or you can make an issue of this and make an enemy of me. I think between us we have enough enemies, don't you think?"

Huang was speechless, as if nobody had ever dared to speak to him that way before. Taylor knew Huber handled him right, and he was following in his footsteps. Huber was a great loss to them all that they could not afford, but he had to move past it now and do the best he could.

"I won't be stopped, Admiral, you know that. All I want is the chance to fight. So will you stand with me or not?"

He offered out his hand in a sign of good will. Huang looked to his staff but finally took it. Taylor gripped his hand firmly and hauled him in close.

"We need you to be the man now. Not any old man. Not a shitty Admiral or a lay about, we need a great man. I think you can be that, and I'll help you be one. Have you got it in you to fill Huber's shoes, and be the man to lead our fleet home?"

Taylor leaned back and looked into his eyes, waiting for a response while still holding the handshake firmly. Huang was still a little stunned by the whole experience but slowly nodded in agreement.

"You are a hero of our whole world and race, Colonel. If you will serve me as you did Admiral Huber, I will gladly have you command the first operation that marks the return to Earth."

Taylor smiled in response and withdrew his grip to salute the Admiral. He was bareheaded, but he gave a salute anyway, as a sign of the respect and the future they had together.

"Assemble your troops, Colonel. You have a few short days to prepare for this operation, and I wish you every luck."

He then turned and strolled away; confident in the notion he had maintained his hold on command. Taylor could see some potential in the man, and he prayed he could be the man they needed him to be. He'd never thought of the Chinese as fighters. He'd heard tales of their bravery in the wars, but he'd never seen it with his own eyes. And even though he had marines in his unit of Chinese descent, he had always believed they were the fighters they were because of American training.

More and more he was realising there was little of America left in his life. Half of the Inter-Allied Regiment were British, plenty more were from Continental Europe, and an increasing number from the East. They had assembled as a Regiment formed from two nations, but they were ever more becoming a multi-national outfit.

Taylor was raring to go, and the days passed quickly when he found himself standing before his unit that had assembled ready for Irala's briefing. They had received nothing from their allies in the passing days, but Taylor wasn't bothered. Something deep down told him he was right to trust them, and practically, he knew he had no choice. Most of the Inter-Allied formed there had served beside him for at least a couple of years or more. Twenty percent were new recruits that had been training since leaving Earth. Green, but well trained.

They were all surprised to see Irala approach on top of some kind of a hovercraft with another of his people. They wondered if this was perhaps only the second time they had ever seen him for real, the other occasion when he fought the Krys when they first met. The alien stepped off the craft, and Taylor could see he was indeed real.

"Colonel Taylor, are you ready to strike at the defence platform?" he asked.

"Yes, other than the fact we don't know what it looks like, the strength on board, or what our job will really be. What do you need marines for anyway? I figure we'll jump into the system, blow the hell out of the platform, and get out."

He could already see that Irala had other plans.

"The Krys once made you destroy your own weapons platform in a cruel turn, would you not prefer to insult them further?"

"What did you have in mind?"

Irala smiled. It was the first time he had ever seen the expression.

"You are a Marine Colonel, a fighter, and we have a part of this plan especially for you."

"As long as it involves us killing those bastards, I'm in."

* * *

The days had passed and the continuous training had never been focused enough, for they still didn't know the plan of Irala. He stepped up before them to address Taylor.

"Embark, and follow us."

Taylor was shocked. He reached forwards and grabbed Irala's arm. The alien spun around in surprise.

"You want us to follow you, without a clue of what we're doing?"

"I assumed you had discovered that for yourself by now."

Taylor didn't know what he meant.

"What would you do, if you could do anything with that weapons platform?"

Taylor thought for a few short seconds before blurting out a response. "Board it, turn the weapons system on enemy targets on the ground, and then destroy the platform itself before leaving."

Irala nodded in agreement. "It took you this long to understand?"

Taylor shook his head in amazement. "Briefings normally involve sharing information, you know," he replied.

"And we expect more. Embark and prepare to lift off."

Irala turned and left without another word. Taylor had never experienced such a passive command before, and yet felt compelled to go along with it. He liked these new aliens. He liked their no nonsense approach, even if that did frequently mean he was lacking information. He turned to his unit that were assembled and waiting a long briefing.

"Are you ready to kill those bastards who took our homes?" he bellowed.

A roar of agreement followed.

"Load up and let's move!"

Nobody moved for a moment; they expected so much more.

"We've got Krys to kill. Load up, let's go!" he added.

They still looked surprised, but it was all they needed to hear, and they leapt into action. Parker was the only one to stop in front of him.

"You know this is crazy?" she asked.

"As crazy as leaving our world? As crazy as finding a second alien race?"

Her face slowly broke into a smile, seeing where he was coming from.

"Irala and his people are giving us the means to stick it to Erdogan and his armies. I'll take those odds, no matter how long they are. Will you stand by me, as I need you to?"

She didn't say a word. She only reached forward and

kissed his cheek before falling in and carrying onwards.

Taylor's vessel was the Diderot, and half of the Inter-Allied Regiment was aboard, along with many of Moye's own troops acting in defence of the vessel itself. He made his way to the bridge with Jafar and Parker, where he was met with Lasure and Moye, as he was familiar with.

"She looks as good as new," he said to the Captain.

"Nothing like we ever knew her, but we're up and running."

"You're the only man I know who is mad enough to think this mission is a good idea."

"But you trust in me, Major?"

"Enough to follow you," said Moye.

They lifted off from the world and were once more in the blackness of space. He still didn't like it. He never liked leaving hard ground for the emptiness of space, but this time he knew he would see Earth, and that alone was enough to carry him through. They exited the atmosphere and heard Lasure issue a few commands in his native tongue. A moment later a Gateway opened before them, and they powered on through.

It seemed like as soon as they had travelled through it, they were out again and Earth was ahead of them. The blue azure of the homeworld caused a surge of emotion and memory in all who saw it. Not one of them ever expected to see the planet again.

"That's what we're fighting for," stated Taylor.

"The Krys say it's paradise, is that right? Moye asked Jafar.

Jafar seemed as amazed by the sight as the rest of them. For all of their time on Earth, few of them had ever had much time to marvel at it from orbit.

"Well?" he asked again.

"Look at her," replied Taylor, "Doesn't that answer your question? "

Nobody replied.

"Game face," added Taylor, "We've got a job to do. Let's do it."

They watched the weapons of the platform move to target them, but as they did, beams of energy surged from the allied vessels beside them, striking one single point at the flank of the defence grid. In an instance, the weapons of the platform stopped moving and all was quiet.

"It's our time," said Taylor, "Get to the boats, let's move!"

He looked to Moye one last time. "You be ready when we're heading home, you hear? Good chance we won't be coming out light."

His language use was largely lost on the Frenchman, but Moye still understood what he meant from their situation alone. Taylor rushed off the bridge and headed straight for the Mastiff that was awaiting him. He stepped aboard and went straight to the cockpit where he found Rains.

"Still alive, Lieutenant?"

Taylor knew it was the case but still thought it funny to jest with the pilot.

"I'll still be around long after you pass from this world, Colonel," he replied with a smile.

Eddie laughed, but he also knew it was likely to be true.

"Let's get this bird in the air."

"Yes, Siree."

Just thirty seconds later, they were off the cruiser and well on their way to the defence platform. It was an unnerving experience for both of them to be hurtling towards the heavily armed platform that was still fully intact.

"You sure about this?" Rains asked, "There sure are a lot of guns on there that could be training on us in a split second."

"Irala tells me they have disabled the automatic targeting devices, and that manual override will take them twenty minutes or more."

"But they must have other weapons on board?"

"Some bigger stuff yes, designed for targeting large capital ships or ground targets."

"Ground targets?"

He smiled, realising Taylor's intentions.

"You don't need to board that thing at all. You want to turn their guns on them just to rub salt into the wound."

Taylor took a deep breath and then replied with a wicked grin.

"Nice to know there is some justice in life, don't you think?"

"Hell, yeah."

They soared nearer to the platform and could see two enemy vessels moving to intercept them.

"Not liking the look of those."

"Don't panic, Eddie. We'll be fine," Taylor replied calmly.

Rains shook his head in disbelief, but as he did so, beams from their allied vessels surged past them and cut both intercept craft apart with a single volley.

"Jesus!" yelled Rains, "We gotta get ourselves some of those guns!"

"I'm with you there."

Rains took them in on a rapid descent and only used reverse thrust when he absolutely had to. They came in a little too fast and smashed into one of the bulkheads of the station. The thick armour of both the wall and the Mastiff meant there was no damage to either, but they were rocked violently on impact.

"Nice flying," said Taylor sarcastically.

"Hey, I got you here and in one piece, what more can you ask for?"

Taylor rushed to the access door to find the breaching team were already ready to blow their way in. They looked to him for the go ahead, and he simply nodded to show his approval.

"Fire in the hole!"

The shaped charge blew, and Silva was the first one to jump through the breach. Taylor got through not long after and found they met no resistance at all.

"Caught 'em with their pants down," said Silva gleefully.

Jafar stepped up beside Taylor and simply said, "Follow me."

They didn't question his knowledge and followed him. Taylor looked back for just a moment to check if the two nukes had been carried aboard.

"Oh, yeah, we've got a present coming for you," he whispered to himself.

It felt great to be back in their system, and to be taking the fight to the enemy for once. He didn't care how little it achieved. The fact they were even there made it a triumph already. Jafar led them on for a few minutes down multiple corridors and rooms as though he were entirely familiar with the layout. Then they saw movement up ahead. Two Mechs were guarding a large doorway and began turning their rifles to bring them to bear, but it was too late. Six of the Inter-Allied, including Taylor, acted like a firing squad and swamped them with fire before they could get off a shot.

Jafar carried on running towards the door. He reached it, placed a breaching charge at one side, and ducked back until it blew open. They rushed in with weapons and shields at the ready, finding fifteen Krys crew working at consoles. None of them wore armour, and they froze on seeing the humans enter. The Inter-Allied froze too; they didn't know what to do when confronted with unarmed enemy.

"Kill them all!" Taylor commanded.

The Reitech rifles roared, and carefully aimed bursts struck each of the creatures before most could even get out of their seats. The room fell silent, and nobody felt any satisfaction at executing the enemy. Taylor turned to Jafar.

"This is your rodeo," he stated.

Jafar went right to the consoles and started to go through procedures.

"Get those nukes set to go!"

He looked around and couldn't believe it was all happening so smoothly. It was like the good old days of fighting Karadag and even Demiran.

"We've got incoming!" Parker shouted.

Taylor rushed to the doorway. Flashes of light were coming from one of the corridors ahead where they had posted guards. They were now retreating back towards them.

"Form up!" he ordered.

There was no cover at all, so they were relying on their shields and weight of fire alone. Ten at the front knelt down, and more than that with Taylor stood over them. The resemblance to Napoleonic or Civil War tactics was not lost on him. He only wished Jones had been there to be so amused by it. The two guards fell back and took cover either side of the opening to the corridor, and the Mechs came storming into view.

"Fire!" Taylor shouted.

They might have looked like something off a battlefield a few hundred years before, but they certainly didn't shoot like it. Automatic gunfire soared down the corridor into the creatures. Two-dozen rounds immediately cut down each one that came into view. Those that were left stopped coming and ducked back for cover after seven of their troops lay dead.

"Finished."

Taylor turned to see Jafar next to him.

"Have you overridden the controls?"

"Scrambled yes. It would take more than thirty minutes to undo what has been done."

Taylor rushed forward and launched a grenade down the corridor to where the Mechs were dug in.

"Come on, let's get the hell out of here!"

He reached the corner where the Mechs had been, and only one was still standing. It managed to fire off two pulses. One missed, and the other glanced off his shield. Jafar was already on top of the creature and smashed it against the bulkhead. He broke the joint of the creature's lead arm, forced its own weapon against its chest, and pulled the trigger.

"Quit messing around. We gotta go!" Taylor yelled.

Jafar rushed ahead to lead the way, and they were all glad to be following him off the station, as they were all aware what was coming. They reached the ship without any more interference from the enemy and climbed aboard to find Rains raring to go.

"Thought you'd never come back," he joked.

"Get us the fuck out of here!" Taylor shouted.

They sealed the doors behind the last of the marines, and Rains was all too eager to get them on the move, but as they soared away from the platform, he and Taylor were more focused on the rear facing screens. They watched as two heavy weapons on the platform rotated around and targeted areas on the surface. They immediately fired several repeated bursts.

"That made a statement," said Rains.

"Wish we could see the results, but knowing we pulled it off is enough of a kick in the teeth for Erdogan to keep me happy for now."

"What's that?" Rains asked.

Taylor looked at a scanner screen and tried to identify what he was seeing.

"Oh, shit," Rains swore out loud.

They could now see it was two-dozen enemy ships on an intercept course with them.

"Get us home!"

"Working on it, Colonel!"

The Diderot weapon systems opened fire, and their allies did the same, but they knew it was more than they could deal with at that time. Rains brought them in on a rapid descent to the landing bay of the Diderot, and they hit the deck hard before sliding into one of the bulkheads.

"We're aboard. Go, go, go!" Rains screamed down the comms channel.

They waited anxiously because they couldn't see what was going on and could only wait for some news and hope they made it out okay. Taylor glanced back at his team who were all as stern looking as he was. They hated not being in control of their own fate. Suddenly, Lasure's voice came over the speakers.

"This is the Captain speaking. We're home safe, and the defence grid is blown to hell. Well done everyone."

Cheers rang out through the Mastiff as Eddie lowered the ramp, and they found the deck crew cheering them on. Taylor felt the weight of Rains slap his hand on his shoulder.

"We're back, aren't we? Back from the dark days, and back to doing what we do best, kicking ass."

"You're damn right," he replied.

CHAPTER SEVEN

"What on Earth is that?" Becker asked.

The sun was going down rapidly now, and they watched lights flashing across the sky in the distance.

"Are those weapons?"

Kelly stood up and strained to look closer, lifting his rifle to peer down the scope.

"I've no idea. If they are, what the hell are they shooting at?"

"No idea on that either. But you better hope if those are weapons, they don't come our way."

The lights faded away, and they were left in the dusk once again watching the last of the sunlight fade.

"Ever thought you'd end up living like this, in the wild?"

"Never thought I'd end up living on Earth," Kelly responded.

That brought a smile to Becker's face.

"Don't appreciate her till you've lost her, isn't that the case?"

"I can relate to that."

Becker wasn't sure he was referring the their homes on Earth, the Moon, or some other reference, but he knew the result was the same.

"We obviously made a clean break, what do you want to do from here?"

"Find a target and hit it. Something small scale and safe."

"You want to go back on the offensive?"

"What is the alternative? Fade away and hide for the rest of our lives?"

"I just think if we go looking for trouble, we might not survive the consequences again."

They sat back down on the fallen tree that had been the bench they were perched on and stared at the stars. Almost fifteen minutes later, they once again saw a bright light in the atmosphere, but it was closer this time.

"What on Earth? What the fuck is going on?"

Kelly raised his rifle to examine the sight again.

"Looks like a ship."

"Plummeting into Earth? Why? Not like we've got anything still up there, fighting the good fight."

Kelly was speechless while he tracked the object across the sky as it made its plunge towards the surface. It was finally just a few thousand feet off the ground and comparatively close to the lights they had seen earlier.

"No attempt to slow. Looks like whatever it was it's nothing but a wreck now."

"One of our old satellites?"

"No, far too large for that."

"Well, what then? Can't be one of ours. No chance."

"Could be. Maybe someone found a ship and tried to break for orbit, and got shot out of the sky," added Kelly.

Becker wasn't buying it.

"Nobody would be stupid enough to try it, would they? Too many ifs and maybes."

"You got a better idea?"

Becker shrugged. "Never said that I did."

They watched the final descent of the object. It passed out of view in the distance and finally impacted. Although they couldn't see it any longer, the ball of smoke that arose from the site was clear for all to see.

"Whatever it was, it isn't much anymore," said Becker.

"How far would you say that is from us?"

"Why?"

"I'm curious. How far do you think?"

"About fifty klicks, I would guess."

Becker could see in Kelly's face that he was more than just a little curious.

"Oh, no. No, no, no!"

"What?" Kelly asked.

"You want to go and investigate?"

"Don't you?"

"No, no way. Everyone in the bloody continent saw that come down. You really want that kind of attention after we finally got free?"

"So what? A ship or some satellite came down, who cares? I doubt anyone will go looking."

"Who cares? You do enough, so that probably means others do, too."

"If it's friendly, then nobody is going, anyway. If it's enemy then, well, they don't care what they leave behind. The world is littered with alien vehicles that they have no interest in retrieving."

Becker sighed as he took a few steps and turned away.

"Come on, it's the most interesting thing that has happened since we got out here. Don't you want to know what it is?"

"Not really. My life is complete without that knowledge."

"Fair enough. I'm going. I'm taking twenty with me. If we're not back in twelve hours, you move on out, and I don't want to know where."

Becker agreed even if he didn't like it. Engel walked closer to Kelly as he went to walk away. She had been listening in.

"You wanted your chance to see some action and get a rifle in hand, Lieutenant?"

"Yes, Sir."

"Well, this is it. Gear up, we're moving out in fifteen

minutes."

She looked oddly excited by the prospect, and Becker could not help but laugh at her naive enthusiasm as she scurried off to get her equipment.

"You remember when you were that keen?" Kelly asked him.

"No, I really don't. It's simply to long ago to remember. A different lifetime."

Kelly left and found Engel had already awoken Reynolds and filled him in. The Captain stood with twenty soldiers just as Kelly had told Becker he would take. He appreciated the initiative Engel had taken and didn't want to knock her enthusiasm, even if she had stepped far over her position.

"All right," he stated, "you all know the deal. I take it the Lieutenant has explained it?"

"Only that we were needed," replied Reynolds.

Maybe she has got more sense than I gave her credit for, thought Kelly.

"Okay, for those of you that didn't see it. Something came down from orbit just moments ago. I don't know what it is. I don't know if it's alien or human. I know nothing more than what I saw. Now I think that is worth investigating, and that is just what we'll do. Sun's down, so we can travel through the night. Captain Becker believes it's about fifty klicks away. We should be able to be most of the way back here before first light."

"What are we expecting to find?" Reynolds asked.

Kelly shrugged.

"Could be nothing at all, and we must consider that the crash could have attracted more attention than just ours. So we could find people there, human or alien. Be ready for anything. I'll drive the lead vehicle. We take it slow and steady, everyone happy?"

He knew they weren't, but they agreed anyway.

"All right, get to work."

It wasn't long before they were trundling on through the forest in darkness. They ran with no lights at all, only the night vision glasses each of them wore. An hour of that and Kelly had a splitting headache. He wanted nothing more than to tear them off and carry on with his natural sight, but they couldn't risk the chance of damage to the vehicles. In amongst the towering trees, there was almost no light at all now. Engel was in the passenger seat with him, and Reynolds brought up the rear. Their pace was leisurely, but it was at least low profile.

The Lieutenant had not said a single word since they set off. He wasn't sure if she had nothing to stay or was trying to remain professional while on operation.

"You know you can speak," Kelly finally stated, "You won't make any more noise than these jeeps will."

The two soldiers in the back laughed.

"I'm not sure I have anything to say," Engel finally replied.

"Sure you do. We've known each other long enough

now, and I don't know really anything about you, other than you weren't trained for fieldwork."

"Does it matter?"

"Does what matter?"

"Our lives before all this. It has no bearing on anything, anymore."

"Do you dream?" he asked her.

She didn't know how to respond.

"Do you have dreams?" he asked again.

"Yes."

"And are they good dreams?"

"Yes."

"Then they cannot be about the lives we lead today. You dream of how life used to be and all the nice things you used to have to do, don't you?"

"Yes, I suppose so, Sir."

"Then who we used to be has a bearing on our lives, and it isn't wrong we still think of it and wish for all that to still be ours. If all I had to think about were life out in this forest, with nothing more in my life than the pursuit of killing our invaders, I don't think I'd want to go on living."

"But that is our lives now."

"It's what we see and live with, but not how we have to think. They have taken our homes, towns, friends, and families. But they cannot take what is up here," he said, touching his head, "No, they cannot take that from us. Not until they kill every last human being in the universe, and I can bet you that ain't ever gonna happen."

"You really believe that?"

"Lieutenant. Humanity has lasted out war and famine and the most obnoxious of things for thousands of years, what makes you think we will go down so easily?"

"Just doesn't seem any hope, anymore."

"An hour ago you were raring to go and barely containable, why the change?"

"Maybe the idea of getting involved at the frontline was exciting, but now I'm out here, not so much."

Kelly laughed.

"Hey, you're talking to a Commander who spent a long and prosperous career sitting at a desk."

"Really, Sir?"

"You know what I wouldn't give to have that desk back, and my climate controlled office on a peaceful colony with the lowest crime rate known to man?"

"Sounds like a Utopia."

"Yes, it was. The only good these wars have done for me is get me in fighting shape. Well, I'd give that up in a heartbeat to go back to being an overweight paper pusher on his way to retirement."

"But you've become something better, haven't you?"

Kelly shook his head.

"Don't let anyone tell you that. I am what I am today out of necessity, not even a fool would ever choose it."

"So I'm a fool?"

Kelly sighed. "You know that's not what I meant."

He looked over to see she was smiling back, and he realised she was having him on.

"So this thing we're going to, what do you think it is?" she asked.

"My guess is an enemy vessel of some kind. Something went wrong, and it lost power, who knows?"

"Won't they come looking for it?"

"Nobody could have survived an impact like that, so no. What good would it be to them?"

"Then why are we going?"

"Because maybe I'm wrong, and I'm more than a little curious. And maybe because it beats sitting around doing nothing at all."

"So you'd rather risk your life than be bored?"

"Probably, but you're assuming our camp is any safer than where we're going."

It was an unpleasant thought, enough that they stopped discussing it. It took almost two hours more until they reached the marker Kelly had set. It was the nearest he had estimated to the crash site they could get to before going on foot. He wasn't going to risk driving into a nightmarish situation, if that was indeed what was ahead. He brought the jeep to a standstill. There was no need to look for somewhere to hide the vehicles because they could barely see more than ten metres in any direction.

Kelly took his rifle in hand and waited for the others

to gather around. He could feel now just how cold it was. The heaters of the jeeps had kept them comparatively warm, despite the open tops. He could never get used to the feel of ice-cold air and the moisture it brought in the nighttime. Even so, it was feeling more and more like home all the time.

"Here's the deal," he started, "We don't know what's up ahead, and we don't know the terrain. We stick together. Two by two, so that you keep an eye on the man at your side, a metre between pairs, got it?"

He knew it was far from tactically strong, but he wasn't planning to get into a fight. They continued on, and Engel led the way with him. He wondered what they would find, and he knew she wanted him to explain and make some sense of it, but he still had no clue himself. He was weary from the sheer lack of sleep, and he didn't even notice lights between the trees in the distance.

"Stop," whispered Engel.

Kelly felt his body freeze instinctively before going down on one knee. His pulse was racing, and the adrenaline rush made him acutely aware and awakened to his surroundings. There was no danger in sight, so he got to his feet and continued on slowly and cautiously. As he closed the distance, the lights ahead began to blow out his night vision, so he raised the slider up onto his helmet to return to see the world with his own eyes.

He raised his rifle now to use the scope to see a little

closer and could see what he was looking at. Floodlights lit up an area a kilometre wide in the distance.

"What is it?" asked Engel.

The lights appeared to surround a large space ship of some kind, but it was too badly damaged for him to identify much, if anything from a distance."

"Is it human?' Reynolds asked.

"We haven't got anything that big, have we?"

"Not anymore, Lieutenant," said Kelly.

"So what the hell are we looking at?"

Kelly shook his head; he had no idea.

"You two with me, the rest of you, take up positions here, and do not move unless you come under fire."

They carried on through the undergrowth, and with every step kept a keen eye on what was before them. Eventually, they reached a position a few trees back from where the vast chasm had been created from the impact. Ten metre-high floodlights were embedded in the treeline all around, but there was no sign of anything living.

"This looks like a recovery operation, Sir," said Engel.

"Why do you say that?"

"I worked a desk like you, remember. I have seen enough operations on paper. When we lost a 'copter or there was some accident, we would send out recovery and investigation teams."

"And you think they work the same way?"

"Why not, Captain?" Kelly replied.

He peered through his scope now and could see in great detail, with the amount of light being projected. It was still difficult to identify what he was looking at, due to the damage, but he could tell immediately that it wasn't human.

"Krys, just as I thought."

"It's huge, though," said Reynolds.

"Indeed, and I am not sure this is all of it."

"What do you mean?"

"I think whatever caused this to come down was done long before it began to burn up on the way through. Something tore this ship apart, or whatever it is."

"Who though? Not like we have any fleets left."

"I wouldn't like to speculate, Engel, but I don't think we're alone. I don't think this was an accident. Somebody just gave the Krys a punch in the mouth, and it landed hard."

He couldn't believe it, but he found a surge of hope fill his heart.

"Whoever did this, if they can bring something this size down, they must be powerful, far beyond our means."

"Yes, Reynolds, and they're making a hell of a statement."

It was the kind of revelation none of them could ever have believed in, and yet all hoped for when they lay awake at night. Kelly noticed a glimmer of movement and stayed exactly put and watched.

"Don't move," he whispered.

They watched three Krys stroll into view in the distance. None of them wore armour, and several carried objects more closely resembling scientific implements than weapons.

"What the hell is this?" Reynolds exclaimed.

"You were right," Kelly said to Engel, "They're here to investigate. You know what that tells me?"

The two of them looked dumbfounded.

"They aren't sure what did this, and more significantly, they're scared. The Krys don't recover any equipment, no matter how large. Something ruined their day, and they're trying to figure out how and why, I should imagine."

"So what do we do?"

"Add to the list of their problems," Kelly replied, smiling.

"You what? You want to fight them?"

"Why not, Captain? They hunted us down, so let's see how they like it. I want them to know nowhere in these forests is safe. I want them to fear an attack in every moment they are here. We've been scared of them and what they'd do to us for so long, it's time we returned the favour."

He took a look through his scope again. Only a single small craft landed at the site, and no more than the three aliens he had first spotted.

"Go and bring the others up here," he ordered Engel.

As she left, Reynolds moved up to take a better look for himself.

"Can't be all of them, surely? They'd have support, Mechs, something."

"I would have thought so, too."

He sat down against a broad tree base and waited for Engel to return. He knew they weren't even at platoon strength, but he couldn't resist getting his teeth into the enemy. Looking at the group, he could see all their attention was on the site behind him.

"Take a good look," he added, "That's one of theirs. Something knocked it out of the sky, and it sure wasn't us. But what I do know is, whoever is responsible, we need to give them some help. Now I reckon that's an investigative team looking into what happened. We finish them here, and we'll make that bastard Erdogan think there is a combined ground effort that is kicking him in the ass."

"How do we know that, whatever it was... was shot down?" asked one of the women.

"It came out of orbit. That didn't happen by accident or with some kind of engine failure. Their tech is too good for that. And with all that much damage; no this thing was sabotaged in a big way. That's either a very large vessel, some kind of carrier maybe, or a space station, but it certainly isn't of human origin."

"So we don't really know what it is, why it's here, or why they are here, but we're gonna hit them anyway?" the woman asked again.

"The Commander is talking sense. If there is someone else out there fighting back, we should be doing all we can, too," said Engel.

"Yeah, but killing three, and risking us all to do it?"

Kelly looked at Reynolds and then took a deep breath. They all waited for his reply.

"I wasn't asking any of you what you wanted to do. I'm running this operation, and we're hitting the enemy now. Anyone don't like it, they better pack their bags and go it alone."

Reynolds didn't reply.

"All happy?" Kelly asked.

They nodded in agreement.

"Okay, we hit them from two directions. Reynolds, you go forward with your section and dig in. Rest of us will advance round that right flank. With any luck, we'll get into position and be ready to fire before they spot us, but you never know. Be ready to fire any moment if we get spotted. Priority is that they don't reach that craft. We cannot have them escape."

"And if there are more on board? They could just fly on out of here when we start shooting."

"Then assign two of your people to hit their engines the minute they see that happening," replied Kelly in a growly tone, and sounding offended that he had to explain the fact, "Enough talk, nobody says a word now. The next noise I want to hear from any of you is bullets coming out of those barrels, you got it?"

He got to his feet and led half the group off to the flank, moving as quietly as he possibly could. He watched the silhouettes of the enemy in the distance very carefully, expecting them to react in any moment. He knew the floodlighting would blind their night vision abilities. Or at least that would be the case for humans, and hoped they were alike. He felt a branch break under his feet and was met with the wince inducing sound of it cracking under his foot. He stopped dead.

Kelly wanted to close his eyes but forced himself to look at the creatures and study them for any sign of movement. There was nothing, and he a breathed out a sigh of relief and carried on. He reached the position he wanted and pointed for the others to fan out and take up position.

The creatures ahead still hadn't moved more than a metre or two in any direction. Mostly, they just looked at the small display screens they carried, and appeared to be collecting and analysing data. He carefully brought his rifle up to his shoulder and took aim at the first one.

"Ready," he whispered, and then finally, "Fire!"

Kelly squeezed the trigger and let off two shots with perfect accuracy. The Reitech rounds met little resistance, passing right through the creature's body. It stumbled and tried to get back to its feet. He followed with another burst and put it down for good.

He looked around for another target, but the other two were down on the ground, so he leapt to his feet and rushed towards the aircraft. As he did so, the engines fired up just as he feared they would.

"Take them down!"

He fired from the hip and kept moving. Tracer fire zipped past him as the others joined in. The vehicle had lifted a metre off the ground when Kelly reached it. The access ramp began to rise as it gained lift. He drew a grenade from his armour, twisted the primer, and launched it at the door as the ramp went up to close. The grenade went high and bounced off the fuselage. It hit the inside of the ramp, bounced into the craft, and the door sealed shut.

Kelly rushed back a few paces. Gunfire ricocheted off the armoured hull, and as it surged forward a few metres, a huge explosion rang out. Most of the craft stayed intact, with only small prices of shrapnel coursing off in different directions. The engines immediately lost power, and the vehicle dropped out of the sky as if tossed off a cliff side. It landed hard just thirty metres away from Kelly, and he immediately rushed towards the crash site.

The door of the craft was slightly ajar where it had partly burst open, and the hull had buckled from the impact of hitting the ground.

"They can't have survived that," said Engel who had

rushed to Kelly's side.

"Let's not take any chances, hey," he replied.

He took a second grenade out, primed it, and threw it through the opening of the door towards the cockpit. The explosion blew out the glass at the front of the craft, and Engel rushed to the breach to see for herself.

"They're dead!" she shouted.

Kelly grabbed the edge of the doorway and tugged on it until it pulled ajar enough for him to step inside. He flicked the torch on that was built into his rifle and studied every centimetre of the interior. There were just two aliens at the front of the cockpit. Caseloads of equipment lay either side of the storage area. He lifted the lid off one where the grenade blast had knocked it open. Inside, he found some sort of electronics box, but it meant nothing to him.

"What is all this stuff?"

Kelly turned; Reynolds had followed him in.

"If I had to guess, I think we were right the first time. I think this team came here for answers. Looks like this wasn't part of Erdogan's plan, and I bet he wants to know why it happened."

"But why send only five? They've got no armour and nothing more than sidearms."

"They weren't expecting a fight. Why would they? A remote location like this."

"But they know we're in these forests playing hell with

them."

"And maybe they don't see it that way. Maybe we're nothing more than a mild irritation, a rash that will eventually fade away."

"I think we just proved otherwise," said Engel through the smashed cockpit.

Kelly smiled. "This war isn't over. Not by a long shot. I don't know what happened here, and I don't know why, but we're in this fight. Not just to piss them off, but we're in it with a fighting chance."

"Jumping to some major conclusions there, aren't you?"

"Yes, Captain Reynolds, and so should you. I said we came out here to keep on fighting. I said we had no chance of survival or winning, and that we only existed to make them suffer. I was wrong. It isn't enough for our people. They need hope. Maybe this is it, maybe it isn't, but they need it. I say human resistance shot down this ship, and that's what you'll say, too. That is the evidence we found here. We're not alone. We aren't beaten."

Kelly could feel that even as he said the words, he began to believe them himself.

"So we lie?"

Kelly shook his head.

"We gather information and intelligence, and we work on it, Engel. This is what I believe happened here. Maybe I'm right, maybe not. But who cares? What if we told Captain Becker there was hope? That the rest of our people knew there was some glimmer of hope for victory, and that we didn't just come out here to prolong our own eventual deaths? This is the most important event since we were forced from our homes in Ramstein. It's about what we believe in, Lieutenant. So what will it be? Will you believe in hope?"

He could see she wanted to believe it, and so did the others.

"When we found the Drachenburg, we found hope and a camaraderie we hadn't seen since the first war. I want that back, and you're gonna help me get it. We're not fighting to lose. We're fighting to win this war. Are you with me?"

A few grunts of approval came before some of them began to understand there was no reason not to think it. Even the faintest of hopes was better than none at all. The volume increased as they accepted what it was doing for their morale.

"Let's go on home with the good news. Let us return triumphantly and with a story of hope. Let's move out!"

He could see and feel the excitement amongst them now as they made their way back to the vehicles and headed on back to their people.

"We're heading home," Kelly said to Engel.

"Home?"

"We have lost enough buildings and towns we called home that they just don't matter anymore. Home is where our people are, whether that's in a bunker, on a ship, or in the middle of the wilderness.

"You really believe that?"

"Why not? Why can't one place on this world be our home anymore than any other place?"

He climbed aboard his jeep and began the long trek back. He felt like a new man on the return journey. The weariness he had felt on the way there was gone now. They had achieved just a small victory tactically, but there was far more to it than that. He had just found a cause worth rising for. When they finally rolled into the encampment, it was almost daylight. Becker watched them roll up with an intrigued expression. More than anything, it was their excitement and joy that dumbfounded him.

"You look like you just won the lottery?" Becker asked the Commander.

"I figure we have."

"So what was so amazing you found out there?"

"Hope," he replied with a smug grin.

"Don't bullshit me, Kelly."

"No bullshit, we got into a fight all right, with no casualties. But the ones we killed were there to investigate a battle we had no part in. Something big."

He had Becker's attention now and milked it.

"Someone shot down one of their vessels, something big, bigger than one of our own carriers, back when we had any."

"Someone?"

"I'd say ours."

"How?"

"I don't know how. I only care that it happened. We aren't the only ones in this fight, and whoever else is out there, they are hitting some hammer blows."

"So what are you telling me?"

"That all is not lost. We're still in this fight. We're still in this war."

CHAPTER EIGHT

Taylor stepped out onto the surface of the Aranui planet once again, but not as a stranger. This time he returned a hero to both sides. Huang and Irala stood side-by-side to greet him, and it was a reminder of the great days of the Inter-Allied victories that were celebrated so far and wide. Cheers rang out from the Navy crews who had gathered all around and many more marines who were amongst them.

"Fantastic work, Colonel, you surely deserve a medal in recognition of your extraordinary bravery and achievement," said the Admiral.

"Save it for when I'm standing on Earth, with Erdogan's head beneath my feet, Sir!" he shouted for all nearby to hear.

He wasn't joking either. He wanted nothing more in life than to see the alien Lord dead at his feet, and he didn't much care how he achieved it.

"You still believe you can kill Erdogan, after having failed previously?"

"You saw that, too, Irala?"

"I was told."

"Yeah, he's a tough son of a bitch, but I'll find a way, even if it kills me."

"Which it may well do."

"Well, you're a bundle of joy," he replied and went to smack Irala's shoulder, but remembered too late that as usual it was nothing more than a hologram. His hand passed through, and he almost fell over as he lost balance. He tried to save himself from embarrassment by laughing it off.

"We just kicked Erdogan's ass, aren't you a little happy about that?"

"It is an important step, but only the beginning. Rest yourself, and tomorrow we will continue our work."

Taylor opened his mouth to speak, but Irala had already vanished. He shook his head in disbelief.

"First real victory either of us have had in ages, and he can't celebrate even a little."

"Perhaps they understand the road ahead rather better than we do," replied Huang.

"Yep, and maybe they need to pull the sticks out of their asses and learn to enjoy the little things in life, and the big things for that matter."

Huang looked shocked at the way Taylor spoke to him and that brought a smile to his face. That only served to make Huang uncomfortable and offended further, but Taylor knew the Admiral had no choice but to accept him as he was.

"Sir, if you'll excuse me. My work for the day is done, and me and my boys have more than deserved a little time to celebrate."

"Preparations have already been made for you," he replied.

But Taylor was already on the move and heading for the bar that had been set up a week before. Only the drinks counters themselves were sheltered inside a temporary structure, and lines of bench seats and tables lay out in the open air. They were beside the lines of ships that were undergoing repairs and refits. But with the dry and warm atmosphere, nobody cared at all. Parker rushed to his side, and he wrapped his arm around her as he carried on.

"Never thought I'd see the day," she said.

"Which one?"

"The one where we celebrated a victory again."

"I know; I'd almost forgotten what it felt like to be on the winning side."

"How'd you think Erdogan is feeling right about now?" Morris asked, striding up to them.

"I bet he's pissed!" Silva laughed, "We just rolled up on his new home and took a dump on his porch."

"Nice," Morris grinned, "That's pure poetry."

"Poetry wasn't a requirement of recruitment into the Corps, Captain."

"Evidently."

Taylor laughed in response. "Fighters and drinkers, that's all we're good for."

"I can think of a few other uses for you," joked Parker.

They reached the bar to find the cups of beer handed out freely. The staff there had been recruited right off the civilian barges; they were a mix of nationalities. Many of them cheered Taylor's name, and he raised his cup to them.

"I didn't think we'd ever see this," Parker said, throwing back her drink.

"I know, look at them." He watched their people celebrate like they'd won the war, "If we go on like this for the rest of our lives, I'd be happy."

"Partying, Mitch?"

"A challenge, a fight, humiliating Erdogan, and then back here to celebrate. I could repeat that every week for life, Eli."

"That's good, because maybe that will be the case. War isn't going to be over that easy."

"I don't know," Taylor said, looking over to the alien vessels that had put down beside their ships, "Their technology is something else. With them, we might be in for a quicker fight than you think."

"Aren't you forgetting something rather significant?"

Taylor looked puzzled.

"Their tech is amazing, but they were beaten by the Krys before, and beaten badly by the looks. Ever stopped to wonder why?"

"Irala told me. It was a numbers game."

"And you think that's all? You think he's really telling you everything?"

Taylor shrugged. "Why wouldn't he? And anyway, the Krys aren't what they were. We may have lost the war, but we smashed their armies. We go back there together, and we're going back strong."

"Yeah, we smashed 'em, and they smashed us, too, but there aren't as many of us left as you seem to think."

"Irala tells me Erdogan has let many humans live. That's a whole lot of potential fighters we have down there. It will be the biggest mistake he ever made."

"Showing mercy?"

Taylor scowled.

"He hasn't shown any mercy. Those people are alive because he has put them to work or he hasn't managed to catch them yet. No, he wouldn't show mercy; he wouldn't know what the word meant," Taylor replied bitterly.

"I meant no offence, Mitch."

Taylor knocked back his drink and tried to get back into the spirit of the occasion. Even hearing Erdogan's name made him angry and on edge. But he put it past him now and went on in a determined manner to enjoy their celebrations. Next thing he knew, he was awaking in a bed in one of the temporary structures and was alone. He had a splitting headache and was massively dehydrated.

"Good morning, Colonel," a voice said to him.

He rolled over. Irala stood at the foot of his bed.

"Jesus, haven't you ever heard of privacy?"

"Yes," he said abruptly.

"Well, can I have a little?"

"I will wait for you outside," he replied and vanished into thin air.

"That's just plain creepy," Mitch muttered to himself, "Can't a guy get a goddamn lie-in just once in a goddamn while?"

He got up and pulled on his clothing and nothing more than a sidearm. It was a rare occasion he felt safe enough to wander freely without his gear. He stepped out into the bright sunlight and felt the heat burning his eyes.

Why? Why so early on this of all days?

"Good morning, Colonel," Irala repeated.

He opened his eyes. The Alien stood beside him. Then he felt something strike him lightly on his shoulder. It was Jafar offering him a flask of water. He took it appreciatively and knocked it back in one. Water dribbled down his mouth and uniform, but it felt so good he didn't care, and he knew the sweltering heat would have his shirt dry in no time.

"What can I do for you, Irala?"

"You asked me to share more with you about our race, and now we are ready."

It was unexpected. "Okay."

"Follow me."

He did so, and Jafar trailed close behind. Irala looked at Taylor, as if about say Jafar could not come, but Taylor beat him to it.

"He goes where I go. You trust me, so trust him."

Irala said nothing and led them onwards, out of the camp. They paced out into the middle of nowhere until Irala finally stopped. Taylor looked around in every direction for some sign of civilisation, but there was nothing but their fleet in the distance. Taylor sighed and wondered if his time was just being wasted.

"You got me up for this? For a walk about the desert?"

He asked as he kicked the sand and felt hard rock just beneath the surface.

"We've known each other for weeks, and still I see nothing but sand. A few ships, you. Well, not even you, a hologram. When are you going to let us in? We are allies."

The ground in front of him suddenly opened up and dropped down in a cascading fashion, forming a stairway like it had when they first met.

"This is why I brought you here." He held out his hand to invite Taylor in.

"Just the two of us? You know I don't lead my people,

right? I'm just a marine...a fighter, that's all."

"It is clear to all that you are far more than that. Your significance to Erdogan alone showed us that."

He pointed down the broad stairway in the rock once again. Taylor looked in warily. He could see lights emanating from inside, but he couldn't see any other way in or out, and he didn't like that fact.

"You remember we are allies, right?"

Irala nodded.

"And you know we pose no threat to you, and neither does he," Mitch pointed to Jafar.

"We invite you in. I cannot promise your friend will be made comfortable, but I will guarantee both your safety while you continue to pose no threat to us."

"That's reassuring," he replied.

"You ask a lot."

"Well, we need a lot."

He went on down the stairway with Jafar close behind. The carried just a pistol and Assegai each, the lightest load any of them would ever carry. Fifty steps down, and Taylor could finally see the ground stretching out into a room. Irala stood in front of them. He turned back to see the hologram was still following them, but it vanished as he looked. He turned back to the alien now in front of him.

"You for real this time?"

He nodded, and Taylor outstretched his hand in

friendship. Irala took it as if knowing the human gesture intimately.

"You know I'm really not keen on that hologram shit. Erdogan uses it to piss me off, and I don't much like being reminded of that."

"Then I am sorry that you are made uncomfortable, but our use of hologram technology is a necessity."

Taylor looked confused. "What do you mean?"

Irala gestured for them to follow him. It was at this time Taylor looked at the room they were in and studied it. The walls and ceiling were one cylindrical tunnel shape, and bands of light were spaced every couple of metres for as far as he could see. It gave such a balanced light it almost felt unnatural. The room corridor was more than twenty metres wide, and he could see others linked to it further along.

There was no sign of text, images, or decoration anywhere; not even cables, switches, or control panels of any kind. The smell too was just as surgically clean as the look. It smelt as if it had been cleaned with violently strong solutions that made Taylor's nose tingle, it was so severe. Despite the clean feel and appearance, it was far from inviting and homely.

"Makes the Fatihi look interesting," whispered Taylor.

"Yes," Jafar said, but made no comment.

They took a bend, and Irala stopped to look at what appeared to be nothing but a black wall. He passed his hand over an empty area of space nearby, and that blackness faded to reveal a transparent glass of some kind. Inside, three of Irala's kind lay on what appeared to be medical incubation tables.

"What is this?" Taylor asked.

"This is why we use holograms. We possess technology far superior to either of your races. Intellectually, we are a world apart, but physically we are...weak."

"Weak? Didn't look too weak kicking ass out there."

"All of our strength derives from advanced technologies."

He pointed to the suit he wore.

"Wearing of this suit, allows me to pick either of you off the ground and throw you across this room with little effort. Without it, I would struggle to push you off balance."

"I get that; we use exoskeleton suits to boost our combat abilities and strength."

"A primitive but effective solution, but far less significant than what I speak of. We require these suits in order to be strong beside your races, but they drain our bodies of energy rapidly. They allow us to do things our physiology was never intended for. We may wear these suits for a matter of hours only at a time before needing substantial recovery time."

"That's a bitch."

"We are a small race. Rich in science, but we are few. We

live long lives, and yet can be killed easily."

"Thousands of years, you say?"

"Sometimes. You asked why we lost to Erdogan's kind. This is why. There were too few of us, and we are forever limited by the time we can be combat effective. We are also more susceptible to disease, and the loss of a single one of us is a major loss for our people. There are less than nine hundred of us left. The losses we took to protect your fleet were more than we can ever afford to lose again."

Taylor felt a shiver down his spine; the personal cost to them for assisting a race they cared nothing for.

"Then why did you do it? Help us," he asked.

"Because some things in life are more important than merely surviving. Some things are worth fighting for, and worth dying for."

"Couldn't have said it better myself."

He looked back at the creatures on the tables.

"So those robots you sent against us, you developed them to fight in your stead?"

"Yes."

"Then why not make more of them? An army of those things could take on the Krys."

"We do not have the resources to build, maintain, and operate such an army."

"Why not? If you can build machines like that, then why can't you build machines to keep on building more of 'em?"

"As autonomous drones they are effective guards, but not as proficient soldiers. Not like you seem to think."

"Well I saw them kicking some serious ass, and nearly ended us two."

"Those were under the direct control of well-trained Aranui operators."

"Ones like you? Sitting inside those robots?"

"Not inside, controlled remotely."

Taylor shook his head, seeing how short sighted he had been. He was starting to understand he was still thinking in old world terms, before their contact with alien races. It had been so much to take in over the years that he forever found himself reverting to old ideas.

"So if you need one of your own to control these things, you can never field many, and I'm guessing you have to be fairly close to maintain a signal with them."

Irala nodded his head slowly.

"The Krys have always managed to jam our communications in combat, so how do you get around that?"

"We lost greatly because of that, but it is no longer a problem."

"You can get around their jamming? That's cost us dearly. Please show us how you do it."

"In time."

Irala led them on to a room with the robots they had first fought. They were lined up, six either side of the room, and Taylor could see doors leading to other similar rooms of the machines.

"You don't have the people to man these things, so build them for us, and let my people drive 'em. We'd take Erdogan's armies apart, without ever having to lose people in the process."

"It would take many years to train humans to control these devices, if the human mind was even capable; and my people cannot risk humans having the power and ability to destroy us."

"Why would we want to do that?"

"Right now, you have no reason to, but in the future?"

Taylor opened his mouth to speak but soon shut it again; knowing Irala was talking sense, even if it didn't help their position right now.

"So you're technologically ahead of us by what, hundreds of years? But you won't risk the few people you have, and don't want to share too much with us? What will you do?"

"Everything we can."

He led them to a room filled with projected displays screens. For a moment, Taylor tried to recognise what he was seeing, and then noticed they were scenes on Earth. Some showed Mech forces at locations he recognised, but others showed humans in communities.

"What is this?"

'This is your world."

"Yes, I can see that," replied Taylor, "but when?"

"Now, or as close as we can get. The images are transmitted through tiny Gateways."

Taylor looked around at the screens and could barely speak.

"So you've been watching us all the time?"

"Not like this. We maintained our distance and only studied your people infrequently. These feeds were dispersed during your last mission."

"When we went for the defence grid?"

"Yes."

"So you've got a whole extra plan going down, and we knew nothing of it? If we're gonna work together, it's about damn time we had some trust between each other," he demanded.

"Not like this. We monitored you from afar. But on our joint mission together, we took the opportunity to increase our surveillance."

"You see, we are allies, and this is the kind of shit that needs to be shared!"

"But why?" Irala asked.

"So we can work together and best make use of our shared resources, and…"

"Why?"

"To win," he replied, "We have to start trusting each other."

"Is this not trust, bringing you into our home?"

Taylor could sense in his tone that they were the first foreign creatures to have ever done as such, and he needed to stop pushing.

"So have you learnt anything new from these new feeds? Do you know who is left? Anyone still fighting?"

"There is still some outlying resistance. Not enough that they could make a difference alone, but still they fight."

Irala seemed surprised by the prospect, and Taylor looked at him to clarify.

"To fight without chance of success? Why not flee or surrender?"

"Surrender? I've seen what they do to humans. Our civilisation would be gone in a year."

"You have encountered far lesser Lords of their people, but Erdogan will not seek to make your race extinct, at least not yet."

"You said before he will put humans to work?"

"Yes."

"But why?"

"If humans work for him like average Krys do, why destroy a useful commodity?"

It was cold, but Taylor took it as some relief that so many could still be alive.

"You said about resistance. Tell me more about them."

"We have identified seventeen areas where resistance is proving effective at hindering enemy forces," he said, pointing to a row of displays screens.

Taylor paced up closer to them and studied each of them carefully. Many of the areas were in countries he had never even been to and meant nothing to him. Most were remote locations, although he instantly recognised New York.

"People are still fighting there? It was flattened."

Only a few landmarks that were still standing allowed him to work it out. The video feed zoomed in to a street where he could see some movement. A handful of humans darted out from the front of a store and vanished below the surface via a subway station.

"How do they keep going on?"

"Wouldn't you?" Jafar asked.

They were the first words he had heard from his friend since descending into the Aranui base.

"Maybe, but it's our job. They didn't even look like regular forces. Probably just a bunch of civilians that have scavenged weapons."

"There are no civilians anymore," he replied, "Only fighters and slaves."

Taylor could tell the concept was familiar to him. There was a hint of bitterness in his tone. He carried on looking from screen to screen. He didn't even know exactly what he was looking for, and then Irala asked him.

"What do you hope to find?"

"I don't know. Hope maybe," Taylor answered him.

He turned back to Irala. "Do these fighters have any

chance?"

"Chance of what?"

"Making it?"

"I do not know what you mean."

"Can they survive, can they keep on going as they are and keep living?"

Irala shook his head. "We believe the resistance elements on Earth will be finished within three months."

"So Erdogan is hunting them down?"

"Yes."

"He can't afford to have any loose ends, I guess...just like us," added Taylor.

"He studied the screens and passed over two that meant little to him, finally stopping on the third. It was a bird's eye view of a few dozen vehicles parked in a clearing amongst tall trees.

"Can you zoom in on that?" he asked, stepping closer and carefully studying the image. The projection drew nearer and was remarkably sharp. The focus closed in on the vehicle in the centre. Taylor seemed to recognise the vehicle, despite damage to its roof, but he could not remember why.

"I've seen that before."

"That location?" Irala asked.

"Where is it?"

"The Black Forest in Germany."

That got Taylor's interest even more, and he continued

to focus on the vehicle as the camera feed zoomed in. There was a person sitting on the hood, leaning back against the windscreen as if they were resting there. But as they closed in, he could see it was a man reading a book. Not an e-reader, but an actual physical book.

"What the hell?"

Taylor could see the man wore Reitech armour, and a rifle lay on the hood beside him in what was a bizarre scene. A helmet lay next to the helmet, and all Taylor could make out was the baldhead of the character.

"Can we get this from another angle?" he asked Irala.

"No. We have to be very careful to avoid detection. This is all we can do, right now."

Taylor looked back to the man. It was the correct location, and the truck looked right.

"Jafar, you recognise that truck?" he asked.

His friend said nothing. Then as Taylor continued to stare at the screen, the man looked up into the sky as if looking almost right into the camera because he knew he was being watched.

"I don't believe it!"

"You know this man?"

"Bet your ass I do, Irala. Kelly is one of the hardest bastards the wars ever created. I should have known he'd still be there and raising hell. He could have come with us, but he told me no. He said he wouldn't leave his home again."

"The very same words some of my people said. None of which survived the experience."

"Three months, you say? You think that's all the time they have left?"

Irala nodded, and Taylor looked back to Kelly once again. The Commander had gone back to his book as if he had no worries in the world. It brought a smile to Taylor's face, but then he thought back to Irala's warning.

"So if we don't do something soon, they're gonna die. That's what you just told me."

"Yes."

"Then it's about time we did something."

"We are not ready to strike against ground targets."

"You just brought me in here to show us that we have friends still alive down there, and now you're telling me we can do nothing to help them? I don't accept that. We went back to Earth, and we kicked ass. We can do it again."

"We risk too much to act now."

"So you'd have us just leave our friends to die?"

"Unless you wish to die alongside them, yes."

Taylor shook his head, desperately trying to find some way to help Kelly.

"I don't accept that we can do nothing. I won't."

Irala remained silent.

"Could you just do nothing? If they were your people down there, your friends. Honestly tell me, would you sit by and watch them die, knowing that's exactly what'll happen? In three months, you say? So we have to sit by and wait and watch every day for that to go down?"

Still he got no response, and he began pacing back and forth around the room. He looked at the screens once again and to the other groups of human resistance fighters around the world.

"They fight on not only for survival, but for some hope that the rest of us will one day go back. What good is it if they're all dead?"

"Only moments ago you believed they were already dead," Irala finally replied.

"Yes, and now I know otherwise. Goddamn it!" he screamed in frustration, but he was getting nothing more out of Irala.

"They at least need to know we are alive and have a chance of hitting back. They need to know there is hope. Do you know what that could mean to them? It could transform the fighting down there."

"What are you asking for?"

Taylor thought on it for a moment, watching Kelly continue reading his book.

"Project me down there. Let them see me and talk to them. Kelly's people know me well, and plenty of others know my face and name. They'll trust me, or as much as anyone can trust a hologram."

"And what will you tell them?"

"The truth."

"And compromise everything we are hoping to achieve?"

"It isn't a compromise to share information with your allies," Taylor spat back furiously.

His face was reddening with anger now at the lack of assistance he was getting. He felt helpless watching the isolated groups of survivors on the monitors.

"All I ask is you put me down there to talk with them and give them some hope."

"That would mean taking you back to your solar system. We cannot project over this sort of distance from here."

"Then do it. Send me in there aboard one of your invisible ships. We can be in and out without a fight."

Irala seemed to think about it for a few moments. Taylor knew there was many more of his kind, and yet he almost never saw any of them. He began to wonder if they communicated by means he wasn't seeing. Irala frequently seemed to consult others with just his mind.

"Please. You have no idea what it would mean to them," Taylor pleaded.

"We will consider your proposal. Return here in twelve hours, and we will have your answer."

Twelve hours, he thought. *A shit load can happen in twelve hours.*

But he knew it was the best answer he could hope for.

"Thank you, Irala. I know you are giving a lot, and I can see you're a good man. I only ask you keep pushing with us for the victory we need."

Irala nodded and led them back to the stairway where they had entered and gestured for them to leave. They took the long flight of stairs back up to the surface and were once again struck by the overwhelming temperature. It hit them like a blow to the head when they stepped into the thick stifling air.

"Do you think they'll do it?" he asked Jafar.

"No."

Taylor was surprised by his response and turned to look at his expression, but his face was blank.

"Why the hell wouldn't they?"

"Because they don't understand how humans think."

"And you do?"

Jafar shrugged. "You value each human. Irala only sees the tactical advantage and disadvantage of going to help them."

"And which do you think is the better approach?"

He shook his head. "The better approach is the one where we get into combat the quickest."

Taylor laughed. "Nice to know some things always remain the same."

As the laughter died down, he began to think more about their new allies and what they had just seen.

"How much do you trust them, Jafar?"

"They have not tried to kill me recently."

"So where's that on the scale?"

"Scale?"

"Of trust?"

"I trust they hate the Krys as much as you do."

"But is that enough? Maybe it has to be."

They carried on back to the camp. Taylor thought about everything he had seen. He had learnt more about the Aranui in that short time than he had in the weeks he had known them.

"Not a word about Kelly to anyone, you hear?"

Jafar looked confused.

"If Irala's people are willing to help us, we can break the news then, but until that time we only risk building hope that may have no foundation in fact. Imagine telling Captain Morris his best friend and Commander is alive, along with a load more of his people, I imagine. Only to then say we can't help them, and they'll be dead before long. They don't need that kind of shit floating about their heads."

"You would lie to protect him from disappointment?"

"I would. Spirits are higher than they have been in months. Since Erdogan first arrived at Earth. I won't ruin that for no reason. Our people need to be at their very best, if we're gonna stand any chance back on Earth."

CHAPTER NINE

Kelly finally lay his book down as the light began to fade.

"You've done nothing but read all day." Becker said.

"Yep," he replied casually.

"And you could do that at a time like this?"

"Why not? We work our asses off. We fight and we survive, but we need time to relax and rest. Not every day need be back breaking work."

"I'm not sure our alien friends would agree with you."

"Well, we can agree to disagree with the barrel of my gun jammed down their throats."

"We've hit five targets since you went out that night. Think it's doing a lot of good?"

"Probably not, but it makes me feel a little better."

Snow began to fall lightly, and he looked up to feel the sensation of the flakes landing on his face. It was a welcome experience at first, but the feeling soon faded.

He was thinking of the kind of winter they were in for. He was looking up at the stars now as the sun faded away.

"What is life, if we can't have a little enjoyment, Captain?" he asked.

"I thought you lived to kill the enemy now and nothing more."

"I told you I was wrong about that."

"Maybe, but perhaps you had it right the first time."

"Incoming!" a voice called out that echoed all around.

The shadow of aircraft appeared thirty metres above Kelly's position. It was flying in complete blackout conditions and had not even been spotted by their sentries using night vision. Kelly instantly recognised the silhouette as a Mech craft.

"Where did they come from?" Becker yelled.

"Doesn't matter now. Grab your weapons!"

He grabbed his rifle, ducked down beside the fender of his truck, and took aim at the craft. But as he did so, he could see the shapes of Mech warriors leaping from the side of the craft and descending towards him. Boosters on their backs lit up the scene and blinded him to their position. He aimed at the nearest light source and fired a burst. He could see one of the lights splutter where he had hit the boosters, and then the creature veered off to his left flank. He knew he couldn't use night vision now with bright lights, and the pulse cannons would only make it worse when they opened up.

Kelly saw several of his people target the creature he had caused to spiral out of control and decided to move on to his next victim. He turned back just in time to see one Mech land a few metres from him, but with its flank towards him. He fired from the hip, and then raised the rifle to fire a few more shots. The creature collapsed lifelessly to the fresh snow on the ground.

The sky lit up with gunfire as everyone who had a weapon brought it to bear. He could only see two craft in the sky, and neither was particularly substantial.

"How many do you think there are?"

"Looks like a small hunting party, Becker!" Kelly replied and turned to engage another target. As he did, he heard one land behind him, and he turned around. Just as he caught sight of the creature, he felt an impact of its gun barrel swung at him like a club. He felt a bolt of pain soar through him. His left shoulder was dislocated from the impact, and he was pinned against the front of his truck.

The beast swung the weapon for him again. He tried to raise his rifle, but the pain was slowing his entire body. The pulse cannon hit like a club across his face and knocked him out cold. When he finally woke, he was on his back in the rear of the command vehicle. Engel was kneeling beside him with his hand held in hers.

"He's awake," she muttered. Tears dropped down her face.

Kelly's vision was blurred, and he could barely move

through the pain. His neck was so stiff; he could only just tilt his head far enough to see Becker sitting beside him. He could feel the side of his face was heavily swollen, and he could taste the iron of his own blood on his tongue. It was revolting, but he was all too familiar with its taste.

"Where are we?" he asked in a croaky voice.

"On the road," Becker answered.

Kelly tried to shake his head as if to say he knew, but it hurt too much. "Obviously," he muttered.

"We're heading wherever they aren't."

It was enough for Kelly. "Did we lose many?"

"Too many," Engel said quietly.

He tried to get up, but he couldn't manage it. He held out his hand to Engel for support. She obliged and helped him upright and then to his feet. As the vehicle hit a rut, he stumbled slightly and dropped himself down onto one of the seats opposite Becker.

"How did we do?" he asked the Captain.

"About as well as could be hoped. We held them off."

"So it wasn't an all out raid?"

"They hit us with small numbers. Maybe it was a scouting party that stumbled across us. Doesn't matter either way. Each time they hit us, our group gets smaller. We can't hold them off forever."

Kelly said nothing, thinking about Becker's words, and the Captain continued.

"You told us all there was hope, but it was all bullshit,

wasn't it? You told us what we wanted to hear, as always."

Kelly looked to Engel, but she shook her head as if to say she had nothing to do with his tirade.

"You made it up, didn't you? Didn't you? Becker pressed.

"And what if I did?" Kelly replied, with a dry throat and pounding headache. He couldn't find the energy to lie anymore.

"These are our lives you are messing with, Kelly, our entire existence. Why would you fill our heads with hope that never existed?"

Kelly coughed to clear his throat and straightened his back. He was starting to get his senses back now and couldn't believe Becker's lack of faith.

"So what, if I told people there was hope? So what, if I never had any evidence if there was any, or if I just hoped for the best? What does it matter? Do you think our people would prefer to know we're fucked?"

"I think they'd rather know the truth, yes!"

"Truth? Are you serious? Truth is we appeared lost through so many of the days of all the wars, and yet we got through them. And here we are today, still alive and still fighting. How can you say that is without hope?"

Becker was silenced now, and Kelly could see he was giving great consideration to everything they had discussed. He turned his attention to Engel, and in her eyes she still had complete faith in him.

"Don't give me that," he whispered.

"What?" she asked in surprise.

"You still believe in all this crap. Don't! I can't take it anymore."

She gasped.

"I was there when you decided to tell this story of events. It wasn't a lie. It was just an optimist's evaluation. I have clung on to that, and so have many others."

"Yeah? And look where it has got us."

"We never thought it would be easy. We just needed to know we were doing all this for a reason; that we were enduring all this with some end in sight. Some hope of a better life."

"But there isn't."

"There is, if you believe in one. Don't give up hope now; we need you, Sir."

Kelly went quiet as the vehicle rumbled on. Eventually, he realised what pain and weariness he felt, and he slumped back down onto the hard floor of the vehicle and went to sleep. He was exhausted and couldn't bear to hear any of it anymore. When he finally awoke it was daytime, and the vehicle was parked with the rear door open. None of the others were in sight. He got up on his own two feet and felt at least partly recovered, despite the aches and pains. He reached the door and found Engel approaching.

"'Morning, Lieutenant," he said.

"Good afternoon, Sir, almost evening," she replied.

"How long have I been out?"

"A couple of days."

"What? Are we safe?"

She nodded. "So far."

He took her hand and allowed her to help him out of the vehicle. The snow was thick on the ground now.

He could tell why he felt surprisingly refreshed. It was the most rest he had gotten since leaving his home in Ramstein, but he didn't feel good about it. He looked around to the faces of those around him. They were grim, and he could tell they had lost hope. He heard Becker's voice yelling, and the Captain came into view.

"You're awake. It's about time," he stated.

"For what?"

"For you to take over the job that is yours. I wasn't born for this. I'll follow you to the end, but I don't want to lead."

"All this shit, and you still want to follow me?"

"It's a sign of faith in you, don't you think?"

"Yeah, or maybe a sign I'm the mug willing to take the job."

Becker smiled, but they both knew how serious their situation was. Each of them was pandering to their audience. Becker shook Kelly's hand as a sentiment of the hand over of power. Those around them clapped, but the excitement soon died away. He reached over to Engel and used her for support to get to his feet.

"You still need to rest," she said.

"I've rested enough."

He stepped out of the vehicle to see the snow had gotten thicker still so that he could no longer see the earth beneath it. He looked around. Various crews were working to fix damaged vehicles and weapons. Without counting, he could tell they were down on both vehicles and numbers.

"How do you think they found us?"

"Becker, it can't be that difficult if they put their minds to it. We're a big group, and the forest canopy only provides so much protection. Maybe they're tracking with thermal imaging, but hopefully not. Maybe they caught a lucky glimpse on a satellite. But I'd say more likely is they are just using weight of numbers. Keep scouting the land day and night, and eventually you'll find us."

"But they attacked with so few, why not amass their forces when they found us and come all at once?" Engel asked.

"Because they don't have to," Becker joined in, "Each time they find us, we lose people and equipment. They whittle us down bit by bit, casualties and losses that we cannot replace, and they can."

"What can we do about that?"

Kelly shrugged. "I never said there was anything. I only said we could try and live and fight as long as we possibly could."

"No hope?"

"Not unless you believe in miracles, Lieutenant. Now a nice warm fire, that is something we can achieve, right now. Let's get it started."

"A fire? You want to bring the enemy right to us?"

"Look at our people, Captain."

"Freezing cold, depressed, and fed up. The fight is coming to us no matter what, so let's not die cold, hungry, and miserable."

Becker couldn't disagree and turned to a few of their people sitting in the back of one of the trucks, huddled together for heat.

"All right, let's grab some wood and get a fire going."

They looked surprised but quickly moved to it.

Kelly sat back down on the rear step of their command vehicle and watched his people go to work with a new sense of enthusiasm. He could see that a little heat from a fire was the most appealing thing in their lives for now.

Twenty minutes later, they had five fires going, and groups gathering around them. They all knew they were making themselves a huge target, but none of them really cared. Kelly held out his hands towards the fire and felt the comfort it brought. It almost burnt his hands to warm his body while his feet were freezing from the contact with the ground.

"You knew there was never any hope," said Becker, "You knew that from the very start, and you told us all that."

Kelly didn't reply and thought on those words, but finally a response came from behind them and boomed, "He was wrong!"

They turned around to see Colonel Mitch Taylor approaching from the darkness between two of the vehicles beside them. Kelly reached for his pistol and drew it as quick as his ice cold bones could. Becker did the same, and before Kelly could stop him, the Captain pulled the trigger.

To all of their amazement, the bullet passed right through Taylor with no resistance or effect at all.

"Nice to know we're still friends," replied Taylor with a smirk.

"What the hell are you?" Becker asked.

The group of survivors spread out in a circle around Taylor. They were curious but wary. All knew his face, but none believed it could really be him. Many looked around as if expecting to come under attack any moment.

"You aren't Taylor. You can't be," stated Kelly, "Taylor left Earth. If he is even alive, he sure wouldn't come back here."

Taylor was surprised by the hostility.

"I was a fool to think you wouldn't have found some way to survive, Kelly, but you'd be just as much a fool to think I'd never come back."

Kelly stepped up closer to him but still kept his weapon in hand. He reached out and touched Taylor. He found his hand went right through the projection, and that led to gasps by many who were watching.

"What is this? What cruel trick of Erdogan's is this?"

Taylor shook his head. "A trick certainly, but not by the enemy."

"You better start explaining yourself or..."

"Or what, you'll have Becker try and shoot me again?"

Kelly shrugged. He realised there was nothing he could do to silence the projection of Taylor.

"Why should we believe you are...well...Mitch Taylor?"

"You'll just have to trust me. If I told you what had happened to us after we left Earth, and how I am back here with you now, you'd never believe me."

"After all we've seen we'd be willing to give it a shot."

"Trust me, you wouldn't. All you need to know is we're still very much in this fight."

"Yeah? Well where are you?"

"I am told you and your people ambushed a group of Krys investigating a crash site not far from your current location, is that right?"

"Damn right. We watched that thing fall from the sky. By the time we got there, it wasn't much to look at."

"Well who do you think brought that down? That was a Krys defence grid platform. That was our work."

"You were right, Commander!" Engel screamed excitedly.

Kelly wanted to believe it himself, but it all seemed too

good to be true.

"Why should we believe any of this? Why should we even believe you are who you say you are?"

"Because when I came for you in Ramstein, and you told me you were staying here, I said I'd back. I told you I didn't know how, and I didn't know when, but that I'd find a way."

Kelly suddenly thought of a way to test Taylor.

"When you left you took one of ours with you. Who was it?"

Taylor smiled in response. "Captain Morris. He was wounded during our last fight, but is in good health and a serving officer in the Inter-Allied until such time as he returns to you."

"Could it be true?" Kelly muttered quietly.

He wanted it to be true with all his heart, but it seemed impossible.

"I want to help you, I really do, and I intend to find a way to do so," added Taylor.

"Why come to us now?"

"What do you mean?"

"Why at this precise moment? We're taking a beating so bad we're almost finished. Had you shown up with a Marine division and ploughed into this fight, I'd be ecstatic to see you. But no, you come here to talk. If you really are you, you were always a man of action, not words, so where are you now?"

Taylor could hear the desperation in Kelly's voice.

"I'd thought if you were still alive, then things would be faring better."

"We are fighters, not miracle workers. There are less than a couple of hundred of us left. What can you expect us to do?"

"We are organising to retake Earth," stated Taylor.

"Fine words, but when?"

"As soon as we possibly can, Becker. I know we can do it."

"We won't last that long," added the Captain.

Taylor turned to Kelly, but the Commander only nodded in agreement with Becker.

"Then I will go to my superiors and our allies, and plead with them to help get you out sooner."

"I'll only leave Earth if we have your word that we'll be back here before my days are over."

"Hell, yes, we will be."

"Allies?" Becker asked.

"It's a long story; just know that the tide is turning, and we are very much back in this fight. You must hold on. I will come for you. I am Colonel Mitch Taylor, of Earth, and you have my word that I will come for you, and I will take back our world from the enemy."

With his final words, the hologram flickered and then vanished into the night. The group stood staring at Kelly. They were stunned and in disbelief, but he could see hope on their faces.

"What does it mean? Is that all true?" Becker whispered to him.

"Look at them all. They want it to be. They need it to be. If it had been any other person who turned up and wove a story like that before us, I'd call it bullshit. But Taylor, he's the one son of a bitch in this universe that could make it happen."

Becker smiled; the first time Kelly had seen him do so in some time.

"I've heard so much about Colonel Taylor and his Immortals, but I'd never seen him in the flesh."

"You still haven't, Engel," replied Kelly, "but you might just yet."

* * *

Taylor stepped down from the podium from where he had been projected. It was a bizarre experience. He stood atop a circular plate that shifted like a treadmill in all directions as he moved, while the place he was projected was displayed all around him. It was the feeling of being in a video game, and it was also the closest he had gotten to being on Earth since they evacuated.

"Did you find what you were looking for?"

"Kind of, Irala. I found friends that are still alive, but they won't be for much longer without our help."

"You knew Commander Kelly was down there when you saw him on the screen."

"Yes, and now I have seen him with my own eyes, or kind of, whatever! I spoke to him, and he told me how things are down there."

"And could you have expected them to be any better?"

"I guess not."

He rushed out, heading to the exit of the room but stopped at the doorway.

"You know we call our world Earth. What do you call this place?"

"Onesaka."

He nodded and carried on out to the surface of the planet once again.

Onesaka? What in the hell does that mean?

The question soon left his mind. He was going to the headquarters that had been established on the ground, not far from where many of their ships were still undergoing work. It was clear that many of them would never leave the surface again, and were now nothing more than accommodation for their crews. As he headed for the HQ, he found Silva walking towards him. He continued on by his side.

"Been looking all over for you, Colonel."

"I've been a little busy."

"Admiral Huang has been asking all sorts of questions."

"What did you tell him?"

"The truth. I don't have a clue what's going on."

"What's going on is we have people still alive and fighting on Earth, and I intend to find a way to keep some of them alive."

"What? But how?"

"I don't know. I guess it isn't so easy chasing down guerrilla forces as it is taking armies on."

"What are you gonna do?"

"I'm gonna press Huang for some help."

"Well, good luck, Sir. He is never in the best of moods in the times I have seen him, and he's gunning for you."

He passed through into the headquarters and went right up to Huang's office where he was shown through immediately.

"Colonel Taylor. I am told you have been meeting with the Aranui alone. Is this correct?"

"Yes, and..."

"And nothing!" screamed Huang, "You are a Colonel in my fleet, and you will show respect to your superiors!"

Taylor shook his head and wished that Huber could still be with them. Huang was fuming, and yet he knew there was nothing he could do to Taylor; he needed him too much.

"From now on, any contact you have with the Aranui will be made with two of my representatives present, and must be organised and authorised by me, personally."

"Admiral, we're living on the planet beside them. This

isn't some nation the other side of the world. They walk among us and talk to us. I cannot choose when and where they come to me."

"But you will contact my liaison officer before discussing any matters involving the war effort, and must be escorted when travelling off base."

Taylor shook his head.

"You don't agree?"

"It's not for me to agree. Irala and his people still don't trust us. It has taken this long for him to allow me into their lives."

"So you are refusing my order?"

"I'm saying it's not my choice to make. This is Irala's world, and it's awfully good of him to let us stay here and to fight beside us. We can't start telling him what he can and can't do in his own home. Would you be happy if he came here or aboard your vessel and began telling you how things are gonna happen?"

Huang was silenced.

"We live in strange days, Admiral. Things can't always run by the book because our methods of conduct were written before we even knew another race existed, let alone a second one. There is no protocol for this. I will do all I can to include your people with any contact I have, but ultimately, it isn't my choice to make."

Huang seemed to accept the situation now it had been explained to him. It was clear none of his own people were willing to do so.

"Now, I am here to speak with you, Admiral. I came to share information I learnt from our allies, information that is important to us all."

Huang was fixated on Taylor and hanging on his every word.

"Irala's people put surveillance devices into the orbit of Earth last time we were there. The information they can collect is only limited, for risk of being detected, but the important thing is, there are people still alive down there. Not only that, some of them are still fighting."

"That was inevitable. We knew the Earth would fall. It would not happen overnight. It would take weeks, months, or maybe even a year. I should imagine they aren't far from finished now."

There was no empathy in Huang's voice at all, and Taylor could see he had accepted the deaths of all who had stayed behind.

"I know some of the survivors, Sir, and I went down there and spoke to them."

"What? How?"

"That doesn't matter, right now. What matters, is there are groups of resistance that are still fighting, but they haven't got long now. Some of them are my friends."

"And what would you have us do about it? We left Earth to save as many as we could."

"Yes, and now we have allies and the technology and

ability to fight back."

"We are not ready to start the fight back for Earth, Colonel, far from it."

"That's why I want to go in, Sir, and rescue those we can. They could be valuable fighters that we could make good use of. Leave them down there, and it guarantees their deaths.

"I am sorry, Colonel, but we cannot risk an operation this early. We cannot take the losses that would likely result in any kind of rescue attempt."

"I can't leave them down there to die. I won't."

"That is precisely what you will do, Colonel. You knew their fates were sealed when they stayed behind."

Taylor shook his head in disgust and stormed out towards the door.

"You won't go after them, Colonel. That's an order!" Huang shouted.

But Taylor didn't slow down or respond. He left the building, fuming with anger.

"Guess that went well," said Silva.

"Kelly is alive. He's one of them. Captain Becker, too."

"You know this for certain?"

"Yes, I've seen them, talked to them. Not sure they believed it was really me, but never mind."

"What are you gonna do?"

"Not leave them there, that's for sure, but the Admiral doesn't see eye to eye on that. Irala doesn't seem to keen to help either."

"Then what?"

"I don't know. I need time to think."

"Get some chow in you. That'll help."

He agreed, and they carried on to the chow hall, to find many of his people there. He acknowledged Parker with a smile, and then noticed Morris striding towards him with purpose. The Captain rushed right up to him and punched him hard in the jaw. It was hard enough to snap Taylor's head to one side. He shook his head in disbelief.

"As if there aren't enough people who want a piece of me in this life, now you?"

"My people are alive and still fighting, and you've known this for God knows how long?"

"Since this morning."

Morris didn't seem to believe him.

"You have my word. I only kept it from you until I could know for absolute certainty, and also have a plan for helping them out."

"Well, do you?"

Taylor sighed. "I'm working on it, but I'm not finding a lot of interest in the idea."

"You have to find a way, Colonel. Promise me."

Morris stretched out his hand and placed it on Taylor's shoulder.

"You know we owe it to him. He'd do the same for us were our positions reversed."

"Huang is concerned that we risk too much too soon."

"I don't give a shit what he says. He isn't one of us, and he has no more reason to care for our people than Irala and his lot."

"If we are gonna do this, we need help. I don't mean a few hundred marines and one ship. I mean real help. We need the fleet on board, and we need those ships the Aranui use."

"Then find a way, Colonel, I beg you."

Parker handed him some food, and he sat down in a world of his own, thinking it through. Suddenly, halfway through his food, he stopped and got up.

"What is it?"

"I've got it, Eli. I have a way."

"Way to what?"

"To get people to act. If the fleet knew what I know, they'd want to help."

"You're talking about going directly against the Admiral's orders. You're talking about a coup...mutiny."

"Or it'll shame Huang and force his hand to go along with it."

"It's a pretty big gamble, don't you think?"

He didn't respond. He simply rushed off out of the room and headed to the Diderot. Jafar and Parker followed close by.

"You sure about this?" she asked him.

"You know I am."

He reached the ship and found Captain Lasure at the loading ramp, overseeing the appointment of new crewmembers.

"Colonel Taylor," he said with surprise and familiarity, "What can I do for you?"

"I need your help."

Ten minutes later, they stood aboard the bridge of the vessel, and Lasure sat uneasily in his chair.

"You know this is a bad idea?" he asked Taylor.

"No, it's a risky idea, but not a bad one. Can you get this signal out across the fleet?"

"I can, but Admiral Huang could have my command for this."

Taylor drew his pistol and held it casually by his side.

"Then tell Huang I forced you by gunpoint."

Lasure laughed, but he could tell by Taylor's sincerity that he'd be willing to so.

"We can transmit an open message to the fleet, but Admiral Huang can shut us down if you start saying things he doesn't want anyone to hear."

"Trust me, when people hear what I have to say, Huang won't be a problem at all."

"I do hope you're right, Colonel. I don't want to imagine the consequences if this does not go your way."

"What's Huang gonna do, lock us up?"

"That would be customary, followed with a court martial."

"Customs went out the window when we left Earth with a handful of survivors. He can't afford to replace us, anymore than we can afford to replace him."

Lasure looked over to his communications officer and nodded for her to do as Taylor had requested. She signalled to Lasure to say it was ready.

"This is Captain Lasure of the Diderot, hosting a message from Colonel Mitch Taylor of the Inter-Allied Regiment."

Lasure opened his hands towards Taylor as a prompt for him to speak. He took a deep breath, suddenly realising he had not prepared any of what he wanted to say, and so he just opened up with all that he felt.

"I have been back to Earth twice since we have been out here. The second time was just this morning. What I discovered there was that humans still fight on. Most are enslaved, but some still fight, fewer and fewer everyday. I want to get them out. They are our people, fighters. If they have made it this far, then they deserve our help, and we would be stronger for their numbers. Logic would suggest we cannot afford to risk the resources to help them at this stage, but as a human being, I say we cannot afford not to. Our humanity is of more value than anything else. All I ask is that you support our own people. Those who do, please be sure to voice your opinion to Admiral Huang. He may lead this fleet, but the future of humanity is in all our hands. Just ask yourselves, would you want to know there was someone out there coming to help you, if you were left all alone to fight against an enemy as terrifying as the Krys? That'll be all. Taylor out."

He looked to Lasure and then the rest of the crew. They were all staring right at him in astonishment.

"Colonel. If we ever get into a deep dark hole, I want it to be you who comes looking for us," said Lasure.

CHAPTER TEN

"Colonel Taylor! You are ordered to stand down. You are under arrest!"

Taylor shook his head. He suspected it was coming, but he had hoped Huang would see sense. He was still on the bridge of the Diderot, with a crew now utterly devoted to serving him and his plan.

"Distribute firearms and prepare to defend this ship!" Lasure ordered.

Silva, Parker, and Jafar were all of his own unit Taylor had with him, but he did not fear a thing.

"He has to do this, you know," said Parker, "or he looks like a weak idiot. Can't have a Marine officer telling him what to do."

"If he doesn't have the balls for the job, then I'm sure we can find someone better suited," snapped Taylor.

"Mutinous once again, Mitch. We're too used to getting

our way, but it can't always be the case."

"I don't want my own way. I want the people around us to do the right thing."

"Colonel Taylor!" a voice echoed from a loud hailer and piped in through the cameras on the hull of the ship. He instantly recognised it as Huang's voice. A moment later, Lasure had a screen displayed before them, showing the Admiral and twenty of his staff and marines standing at the entrance ramp to the ship. "Colonel Taylor, I am ordering you to report to me immediately and explain your actions!"

"Such a schoolboy," remarked Taylor.

"Colonel Taylor, get down here now!"

Taylor shook his head. "I have to go down there."

"He'll arrest you. I can't see you go behind bars again," pleaded Parker.

"He can't lock me up. He can't afford to. He's just trying to save face and stop me doing what I'm about to do."

"And when has anyone ever succeeded in stopping you?" Silva asked, rhetorically.

Taylor looked around to everyone on the bridge to see if they would stand beside him. There was not a hint of hesitation. He got up and went to leave the bridge, and half of those on the bridge followed him. He stopped and turned to them.

"You don't have to fight this fight with me."

"Go on, we're right behind you," said Parker.

He nodded in gratitude and carried on leaving the bridge. As he exited through the main door, he found the crew of the vessel lining the way for him. They were still and silent, but as he stepped off the bridge, they began chanting his name.

"Taylor, Taylor, Taylor!"

He knew he had the support of the people, and he strode confidently down to meet the Admiral. Finally, he stepped out onto the ramp that led down to the ground where Huang stood. The Admiral tried to appear confident, but it was clear to Taylor he grew ever more uncomfortable by the power Taylor held over all around them.

"I cannot allow you to go on like this," stated Huang.

"I don't believe you have a choice," replied Taylor smugly, "All I want is the best thing for humanity. If you are willing to stand in the way of that, then you are not my ally, and you are not one of us."

"I am the Commander of this fleet, and as a result, the leader of the human race, and..." Huang continued, but Taylor interrupted.

"But this isn't the entire human race, is it?" Taylor hollered, "This is what we left with, but it isn't all. You know it isn't all. I want to bring back our own, and you want to shoot me down. You don't have that right!"

"I am the commander of this fleet," replied Huang.

He went silent and seemed to hope that statement would end the argument, but it only made Taylor shake his head in amazement.

"You weren't chosen to lead this fleet. You are the Admiral of the Chinese fleet. You have no authority over the dozens of other nations among us. You can earn our respect and lead us the right way, or you can leave the job to someone who is capable and able to do it."

Huang didn't reply for a moment, and everyone within twenty metres was silenced. They waited and watched for a response from either of the men. Finally, Huang turned to his own marines.

"Arrest the Colonel!" he shouted for all to hear.

The Chinese troops began to move forward, and Taylor didn't move an inch.

"Don't move!" Lasure ordered, and he paced down the ramp, with pistol in hand, and several of his marine detachment at his flanks.

"Captain, you are ordered to step down!" Huang shouted.

"As the senior French Naval officer in the fleet, I am assuming command of my nation's Navy and do not owe you anything. If any one of you steps aboard this vessel without invitation, it will be judged as an act of war!"

Huang couldn't believe what he was hearing, but his marines had already stopped and looked back to him for confirmation. They looked uneasy, and Taylor only made them feel more uncomfortable, as did Jafar towering over him.

"Admiral, do you want a fight here, or do you want to do the right thing and go to bring our people back?" Taylor asked.

"That is not your decision to make!"

He ordered something in Chinese, and the marines seemed to hesitate before finally moving forward against Taylor. They approached with shields and Assegais drawn, but using them as batons without them being powered up. The first came at him with remarkable speed and accuracy, and he narrowly avoiding the weapon with a side step and threw the man towards Jafar. The man struck Jafar like he had hit a brick wall and fell flat before him.

"Is this what you want?" Taylor shouted to Huang.

A rifle fired in the air, and several shots followed it. It brought everyone to a standstill. They all look for the source and found Captain Morris, with several of the Inter-Allied at his side.

"Admiral, we are going to Earth, whether you like it or not!"

As he said it, a dozen Chinese marines approached to join their countrymen. They held rifles at the ready. Taylor could see it was escalating way out of control. He stepped forward alone and placed himself between the two sides.

"Enough of this!"

But even as he said it, the sound of rifle fire rang out amongst them. Nobody could tell who had fired first, but both sides were quick to pull the trigger. Several dozens shots were fired as Taylor ducked down beneath the fire, yelling for them to stop, but it had little response.

Reitech rounds zipped overhead until finally a bright white light flashed among them. It was blinding and brought the gunfire to an immediate halt. Taylor was sheltering his eyes through the flare. As it finally died down, he stood up and looked for the source. Irala and two of the Aranui stood beside the Admiral. As the humans on both sides of the affray stood up to look at him, they heard the sound of heavy footsteps hitting the hard ground around them. Three of the Aranui robots strode into view and took up positions around Huang.

Nobody said a word for several moments as everybody waited and watched for some response. Everyone feared the enemy robots, and it was terrifying to be looking down the barrels of their guns. Nobody moved and nobody fired, and everybody looked to the aliens for them to say a word. Taylor could recognise Irala out of all of them now. He couldn't even say how. It was in the body language and expressions that made him identifiable. He stepped forward and raised his hands in a human gesture to call for peace.

"Lower your weapons!" he commanded.

Everybody did so, as they were too afraid of the consequences of getting on the wrong side of the highly advanced alien race. All looked to them for answers now.

Irala spoke, "Huang, you will assist Colonel Taylor

in his mission to help those humans, your people, still fighting on Earth."

Huang nodded in agreement and mumbled some words.

"Colonel Taylor is our representative of everything humans do while on our world, and you will submit to his authority."

"But he is just a Marine officer, you do not understand..." appealed Huang, but it did no good.

Irala glared at the Chinese Admiral until he was silenced. The alien strode up the ramp towards Taylor; everyone else stayed frozen still. Taylor smiled in response. "So you've come over to my fight."

"I understand your reasoning, and I have seen fit my people understand."

"So your trust in me is as important as my trust in you?"

"Yes, but if my faith in you is false, I will pay a price beyond all you can imagine."

"Then help me prove you were right."

Taylor stood up to address all the humans who were waiting for him to speak.

"We are going to Earth. We are going to help our own people, and we're gonna bring some of them back with us!"

Cheers rang out from the crowd, but Taylor could see he Admiral still looked unimpressed.

"Admiral Huang. We are going to get our people back. Will you lead us on this great mission?"

Huang quickly realised he could no longer oppose the decision, but could still benefit to stand with it.

"Colonel Taylor, we need a competent ground commander to lead this operation. Will you take the job?" he asked.

Taylor smiled as he accepted, knowing Huang had no choice, though he was glad he understood that fact.

"Then I leave this in your capable hands," stated Huang.

Irala approached the Colonel, and that made Jafar anxious as it always did.

"Easy now," whispered Taylor.

"We will help you," said Irala.

"I think I got that."

"You want to get your people back. Tell me how you intend to do so, and I will do all I can to help."

"What I need from you first is information. If we're gonna get Kelly and the other resistance fighters out, we're gonna need a diversion. We need to know Erdogan's location, his intentions, and the strength of his forces. We need every piece of information you can get."

"But what are your intentions, what would you have us do?"

"I need to lure Erdogan into a trap and bring their forces into chaos. I want to rescue our own people. If any one of those things works, then we will have succeeded. Do you see what I am getting at?"

"Then come with us. Both of you," Irala said to Taylor

and Huang.

He led them out to the open plain and the stairway below the surface. Troops loyal to both men followed them to the entrance, stopping when waved off by the two officers.

"You wanted in on this, Admiral, now is your chance," said Taylor.

Huang looked uneasy, but he followed Taylor and Irala in, anyway. They were led into the same observational room where Taylor had first seen Kelly. This time the screens focused half on groups like Kelly's, and half on substantial enemy locations. Taylor squinted as he recognised something on one of the screens.

"That is you, isn't it?" Irala asked.

Then Taylor realised he was looking at the statue of himself that had been erected in Paris during the rebuilding of the city. He was amazed it was even still there, and he could see Mechs and their drones parading past it.

"Why are you showing me this?"

"This is where we believe Erdogan is. He has established a base in Paris."

"Right there? Paris was a central point of the fighting through much of the wars. It was a city that held in defiance of their armies, and that bastard Erdogan knows it. That statue of me was put there for a reason, and he's pissing all over it."

"He is trying to make you angry?"

Taylor nodded and could feel his blood boiling.

"Then his plan is working?"

"Yes, but not in the way he wants it to. He's making a point that we can't touch him. But all that's doing is making me more determined to take back what is ours."

"Krys forces are mostly amassed at your former capital cities. At least the ones that still remain."

"So they've just take everything, they have taken our lives?"

"Only temporarily, Admiral," Taylor snarled.

"How many troops does he have there?"

"It is hard to say for certain, but many."

"How many is that?" Huang asked.

"Many thousands."

"What? Tens of thousands, hundreds of thousands?" Taylor demanded.

"Yes," Irala replied dryly.

Well that's a big fucking help, thought Taylor.

"Taylor, you want to go back to Earth, but even with our new allies, we cannot defeat Erdogan."

"We can't defeat his armies, no."

"Then what is this all for?"

"Erdogan," he replied, "Erdogan is what is holding it all together. When I killed Demiran, his armies folded around us. Most surrendered outright. Erdogan is even more significant to them. We kill him, and we end the war outright."

"You're sure of this?" the Admiral asked.

"It is true," replied Irala, "We have seen this before. We once tried to kill Erdogan ourselves, but failed. It cost us dearly, but it was a price worth gambling."

"They failed! How can you expect us to succeed where they failed?"

"Have a little faith, Admiral."

"Faith? In what?"

"In ourselves. If you are aiming to lose, then you'll do just that!"

Huang said nothing. Taylor turned to Irala to see if he had anything to say, but they both now seemed to be waiting for Taylor to take the lead. He knew the Army or Marine brass wouldn't be too happy about it, but he'd been given the reins. He didn't want them, but he saw an opportunity, and he was going to do whatever he had to now.

"I thought you wanted to go after your friend, the Moon Commander?" asked Huang.

"No, I said I'd go back for him, but right now, the best thing we can do is start hitting Erdogan as hard and as often as we can. The resistance movements are stirring up trouble, even if they aren't inflicting major casualties. They can survive and keep on going, providing we take the pressure off them. For now, I want to know a few targets that are weak enough for us to hit hard and fast, but important enough to that alien bastard that he can't afford to lose them. Find me those targets," he said to Irala, "And lastly, find Erdogan. Find him, and we can end this."

"When do you wish to depart?"

"Find us the targets, and then we go."

"It is your planet."

"And this is your surveillance, your technology. You know what you are looking at."

"Colonel, last time you went to Earth, you were confronted with an enemy fleet that you could not hope to face. We are not ready for that fight," Huang pleaded.

"Then the fleet will drop us in, and then jump out until we're ready to leave. You are looking for problems, Admiral, but what we need is solutions."

He looked back to Irala. "I'm a marine, a fighter. Get me down there, and let me do what I'm best at."

He strode out of the room and headed for the surface, with the Admiral close at his heels.

"You're putting us entirely in their hands. Letting them call all the shots?"

"I'm not putting us into anything. You will not be going on this operation. And do you honestly think I'd risk the lives of my people, if I thought they couldn't be trusted to do this right? Let's see what Irala comes up with and work from there. In the meantime, I'll get my people ready to go."

"What do you need me to do?"

"Assemble marines ready to fight. I'll need about a thousand of the best to work alongside my regiment."

"Your regiment? Don't you have just a few hundred men at your command now?"

"Yes, and they do the work of two regiments. Just get me the resources I need."

They stepped out onto the surface. The Chinese marines stood glaring at Jafar's every move and looking nervous.

"Come on, we have work to do," Taylor said.

The three of them strolled off quickly, leaving Huang still trying to negotiate with Irala. Taylor could hear him failing miserably and that brought a smile to his face.

"The Admiral, is he up to this?"

"No, Parker. He's not a bad or evil man, but he's no leader."

"So what can we do about that?"

"We? You mean what can I do about that? Nothing at all, Jafar, these things have a habit of sorting themselves out. There are enough people in this fleet who have a hunger for power that they'll soon come looking for it."

"What do we do now?"

"Get as ready as we can be, Parker. How are the new recruits doing?"

"Well considering, but they aren't ready for the field."

"Then get them there."

"You want them to go into a crazy operation like this?

They're green."

"Yeah, you remember the first time we saw Mechs? You remember that time on the Lunar colony? All the training in the world didn't prepare us for that. They've had the best training that can be had, anymore. Everything else will come in time."

"If they survive the experience."

"Well, if they don't, then that saves training them any further, doesn't it?" he joked.

They both knew it was a risky move, but they needed the manpower.

"Are we gonna get some of those Aranui robots to fight beside us?" she asked.

"I have no idea, but we sure could do with them."

"Then shouldn't we at least run some training exercises with them?"

"In an ideal world, yes. But this isn't an ideal world, is it? Get on those recruits, and sweat them."

"Aye, aye, Sir," she said as she peeled off.

The sun was going down, but Taylor took that as no excuse to go slack. He carried on to the Diderot and strode up onto the roof, sitting down at the highest point he could reach. Many of the crews had stopped working for the night, and the only hive of activity was at the bar.

"What would you do?" he asked Jafar, the only one who had followed him up there.

"Fight. As soon and often as we can."

"Do you want to fight to take Earth back, to kill Erdogan, or just because you like to fight?"

"Everything."

"Well, at least you're honest about it."

"You look troubled."

"I am. Erdogan, I think about him all the time. He kicked our asses last time. We didn't even come close to victory. I wonder how in the hell we are gonna do any better next time, short of dropping a bomb on his head."

"Then do that."

"You don't want to beat him in combat?"

"There is no honour in defeat."

Taylor was surprised by his words.

"So you'd kill Erdogan anyway it is possible?"

"Yes."

"Even if that involved flying this ship into him?"

"Yes."

When the sun rose, Taylor awoke atop the ship he had fallen asleep on.

"You want to know how to fight Erdogan? How to kill him?"

Taylor turned to see Irala standing behind him. He knew he hadn't been there the night before, and that made him suspicious of what their allies were watching and monitoring all the time. He made a mental note to remember that in the future.

"Erdogan is like nothing we have ever faced before.

He's got speed, power, intelligence, and agility. I don't know how I can beat him if we ever come face to face again."

"You want to know how he beat us?"

"Weight of number?"

Irala nodded.

"Why are you not training for this battle you imagine will happen?"

"I don't know how."

"Gather twenty of your best fighters, and go one hundred metres west of the furthermost ship you have here."

"Twenty?" asked Taylor in surprise.

"Weight of number," added Irala.

"But what..." began Taylor.

Before he could get off another word, the alien was gone again.

"I hate it when he does that."

He looked to Jafar, but got no response.

"What do you say, old friend? We've tried taking on Erdogan and got whipped, you willing to listen to these people and try it their way?"

"If they can make us better fighters, why would we not?"

He carried on over to the area of sand where Parker had declared their training zone. She was already working the recruits hard, as the veterans of the Regiment sat and watched under the shade of sun shelters.

"Listen up!" yelled Taylor.

His voice carried far enough that everyone came to an immediate halt.

"Irala says he's gonna show us how to beat that bastard Erdogan if we ever have to face him in person again. I want twenty of the best we have to step this way. Jafar is one. Who else has the balls to stand beside us, and prepare for the greatest fight of our lives?"

Nobody responded for some time when Captain Morris finally stood up to address Taylor.

"Why don't we just nuke him?"

"When and if we can, I will end Erdogan with the press of a button, and none of you should hesitate to do the same. We aren't looking for any glory here. We want to win, and we need to survive. So when the bomb fails, when Erdogan somehow slips us, and you come face to face with him. When you have a chance to end it all with your bare hands, will you be ready? I, for one, want to know that if the time comes that I have to face him, I stand a chance of winning. Erdogan aims to humiliate me, so the likelihood is greater than you might think. I want a chance of winning, but I can't do it alone. So who will volunteer, and prepare themselves for such a fight?"

Silva immediately stepped forward.

"A chance to kill Erdogan? How could anyone refuse?"

Lam and Hall immediately came forward after him, and

others quickly joined them until he had nineteen. Lastly, Parker stepped up. He never wanted to risk her, but was glad of her support.

"All right, then, grab your gear and follow me!"

He did just as Irala had told them and found the alien waiting for them when they got there, and a small ship approached from the west. It was one of the Aranui vessels, but none of them had ever seen one up close with their own eyes. The vessel looked like a small transport or reconnaissance craft, perhaps even a fighter. It couldn't have been large enough to carry more than a handful of the aliens.

The craft came into land so smoothly, and with such precision, it didn't appear real. Once on the ground, a ramp came down, and two of the Aranui stepped out. Behind them two large crates floated under their own power, seemingly under some kind of control by the creatures that led them. They stopped, and the crates lowered to the ground. Irala stepped up to them, and the lids opened, revealing some kind of bizarre looking pistol. Like the Aranui vessels, it looked like a sculpted or spun piece of steel. There was not a button, switch, or even a hard edge in sight.

Taylor picked up one of the weapons and marvelled at its precision manufacture, but could not help but laugh at the shape.

"Looks like a cordless drill," he said. The main receiver

was shaped like a torpedo, leading to a grip with no trigger guard. Then a bulbous section protruded from the lower grip and pointed forwards in parallel with the receiver. Several of the others laughed, but to their surprise, Irala picked up one of the weapons and shot Taylor in the face. He was knocked back into the dirt and incapacitating for moment. His head was spinning like he'd been punched full force in the face.

Taylor tried to shake off the effects. His vision was a little blurred, and he felt his strength had just been stripped away from him. As he looked up and his vision began to return, he saw Irala's hand being offered. He took it and was hauled to his feet. He had gotten so used to seeing a hologram, it had never occurred to him that the alien himself was actually present.

"That wasn't a nice experience," stated Taylor.

"This is a stun weapon that has been built for the practice of combat scenarios. It can be calibrated to roughly simulate the type of weapon you want."

Next he pulled a short truncheon-like object from the crate.

"This will represent the Assegai you use. In the practice of combat, it will deliver a stronger effect the harder you strike with it. Both of these training tools take into account the armour penetrating qualities of your weapons. They are as close to simulating a fight as you can get."

"So what now?"

"Erdogan..." said Irala, pointing to Jafar, "Against the rest of you."

"But he's not Erdogan."

"Your Krys friend is the closest of any of us is to Erdogan, and will suffice for this exercise."

Taylor looked to Jafar to see if he had taken offence at the concept, but it didn't seem to bother him at all.

"Take up your weapons, and take up your positions."

One of the Aranui handed Jafar a longer pole weapon that was as tall as he was, and some kind of forearm-mounted device. He strapped it on and a semi-translucent shield device emerged from it. Jafar backed off into the open as the twenty marines took up their equipment and faced off against him. Taylor smiled; it was a game he was already liking. He slipped his pistol out around his shield and fired several shots that Jafar easily absorbed on his shield.

Taylor then rushed at Jafar and kept shooting as he did so. As they closed the distance, Jafar nimbly spun and cut down with his staff onto Taylor's wrist. The shock of the electrified weapon sent a pulse of pain right the way through his arm and made him drop the pistol as he went past.

"Did that hurt?" Irala asked.

Taylor just nodded.

"Erdogan may well have removed your hand with such a strike."

Irala stepped forward and stood between them to address the group.

"Why did you let your leader advance alone?" he asked them.

Nobody had a response.

"Weight of numbers. You must fight as a single unit. You do this in battle against greater numbers, why not when you fight one great target?"

Still there was no response.

"We never had any training in this," Taylor finally said, "When all this started, the concept of fighting in hand-to-hand was all but gone. We carried a knife for emergency use and covert action, but that's about it. All this stuff we have learned we had to so with trial and error."

"Error? Then your first trial just failed. Try again."

He stepped out of the way, and Taylor went back to his group.

"He's faster than I remembered," he whispered to Parker.

"Begin!" called Irala.

"The group of marines opened fire en masse. Jafar absorbed dozens of them with his shield, and quickly and nimbly advanced to one flank. He barged the nearest marine who was launched back from the shield impact. The group tried to head for him, but found their numbers counted for nothing as Jafar drew them into a long column, where he never fought more than two at a time. He struck one after another, cutting his way through marine after marine. The few attacks that landed against him seemed to not transmit any energy at all, and he kept on going. Finally, he reached Taylor, but the Colonel stood upright with his weapons lowered.

"Hardly a fair fight, is it?" he yelled when Jafar stopped before him, "Our weapons have no effect against him!"

"They have a lesser effect. Erdogan cannot be killed so easily. His weapons could cut one of you in half, but unless you strike a weakness in his armour, you will achieve nothing. Again!"

CHAPTER ELEVEN

Several days had passed for Kelly's people on Earth where they had done nothing but wait and hope. Another day was coming to a close, and Kelly looked around to the faces of his people. They all wanted to believe what Taylor had said, but every hour they didn't see some proof of it made them more and more suspicious.

"Sure would have been nice if Taylor actually had given some indication as to when he'd come," said Becker.

"This is war, Captain, how many certainties are there?"

"At the moment, just one. That we're getting our asses kicked."

Kelly cupped his hands together and rubbed them, trying to get some heat into his body.

"I'm not waiting any longer," Kelly said.

"What choice do we have?"

"I'm just gonna die like this. If I die, then it'll be

fighting back. That's what we came out here to do; for the protection it would give us. This place enables us to go on fighting. Not like we did before. We need a return to the hit and run tactics we came here for."

"Hey, if it involves doing something rather than just sitting around here freezing our butts off, then I am with you."

"There is, or was a military installation not far north of here. An old airfield that was overhauled after the war."

"Achern?"

"Yes. My bet is the Krys have continued to use it. It's well located and with an advanced aerial defence network. They could well have put it back into use, should they need it against our own forces. If that really was Taylor and he wasn't bullshitting us, then I bet that base will be operational right about now."

"Okay?"

"Let's hit it."

"Whoa, Kelly, I'm with you on fighting back, but you're talking about a major installation."

"That has almost nothing to defend it against a ground attack."

"Yeah, unless they house a division of Mechs nearby."

"I said it was worth looking at, is all."

Becker looked at his watch.

"It's not too far. We could scout it out tonight, and if it is as you think, then we could plan an operation."

Kelly nodded, and both of them were glad to get up and get moving.

"Reynolds! You're in charge!" Kelly called out.

A number of the group turned in surprise.

"Where are you going?"

Reynolds' voice was shaky, and not just from the cold. It was the fear of having the Commander he relied on leaving them.

"The Captain and I are going to find ourselves a new target, somewhere we can hit the Krys hard."

"You think we're up to that, Sir?"

It was obvious that many of the others shared the Captain's concerns and waited for Kelly to address them.

"Sitting around here, we're just wasting away. I'm gonna find us something worth doing. If Taylor really is coming back, then we owe it to him to stir up as much trouble as we can in the meantime. Berlin, Doyle, let's move!"

He turned and walked to the nearest jeep and climbed into the driver's seat. He'd rather take his truck, but he knew it wasn't suited to the task.

"That's all you're gonna say to them?" Becker asked, climbing in the front beside him.

"I don't think there's much more to say. They need hope, or a victory. I can only provide one of those things, so let's go and find the way."

The two others climbed in behind them, and Kelly quickly got them under way.

241

"Are you familiar with Achern, Corporal?"

"Yes, Sir."

"If the enemy have occupied the base, and I believe they will have, that is our intended target."

Becker looked back to see if she was fazed by the idea at all.

"I have only travelled there once, Sir, so I cannot provide you with much assistance."

"That's okay, anything you can give us would be helpful."

"When I was there, maybe seven or eight hundred personnel were stationed there, with capacity for many more. They maintained and operated approximately fifty combat air aircraft, and perhaps more that I did not see. But it will not be like that, anymore."

"No, but it gives us an idea of the sort of place we're dealing with. What about protection from land attack?"

"To the west and north were bunkers and vehicle traps."

"But not to the south or east?" Becker asked, surprised.

"They were incomplete when I visited, and I do not believe they would have got much further before the last war began."

"So the landing strips are just open for anyone to roll in?" asked Kelly.

"Yes, Sir."

"We're making some pretty big assumptions here," said Becker.

"How so?" Kelly retorted.

"You're working on how things were for our forces. Why on earth would they even use our bases?"

"Why wouldn't they? For a start, look at these weather conditions. No aircraft likes being left out in this. That base gives them areas to house and maintain their aircraft and personnel. We would make use of captured resources just the same. I don't see why they wouldn't. Anyway, we'll know soon enough. Worst case is we find it empty, and we'll see if there are any supplies worth going back for."

"Or they've got some hard core defences set up that spot us from a mile away, and we get blown to hell."

"Come on, Captain. You were all keen to go and do something not so long ago."

He shrugged and couldn't disagree.

"Every time we head out for an operation you get all edgy."

"Just don't like the idea of going to battle in this...car. No armour, no ability to take on armour. No defence from the air."

"We've all had to make sacrifices and compromise."

The journey was uneventful, but as they passed over a hill, the lights of the base came into view. Kelly lifted up his NV goggles.

"Looks like somebody's home," said Becker.

"The solar generators could keep the base powered for decades. It doesn't mean anything." Berlin joined in.

"But that does," said Kelly, as he saw the silhouette of

a Mech fighter heading for the base.

He stopped the vehicle and watched. The aircraft slowed and went in to land down behind a large hangar in the distance.

"So you were right," whispered Becker.

"It's just one aircraft. I want a full picture of what lies ahead."

"We know they're in there, isn't that enough? Wasn't the plan to raid for supplies if there was no one, and raid all guns blazing if there was?"

"No, we need to know if an attack is viable. We can strike hard against a moderate target, but we can't take on an entire army."

Kelly pulled the vehicle off the road that was little more than a dirt track, and found a spot nestled nicely between trees to hide their low profile and easily concealed jeep. He climbed out and could see that Becker looked appalled.

"Where are you going?" he pleaded.

Kelly looked up towards a ridge to his left side and pointed.

"Right up there. It is a damn good vantage point, and I intend to make good use of it."

"Come on, Kelly, we've seen enough."

The Commander looks at Becker's gaunt and pale face and could only smile.

"What's the matter? Afraid of going out into the wild without eight tonnes of metal wrapped around you?'

"Damn right I am. Fighting on foot is for fools and glory seekers."

"Well, we aren't fools. So we might as well go in looking for a little glory."

Becker seemed to calm slightly seeing how lightly Kelly handled the situation and how calm and collected he was about the whole thing.

"Bring your weapons, but stay quiet and stay down. All we need is information at this stage."

Kelly grabbed his rifle and headed up the hill, moving at a slow but steady pace.

"How did I ever end up here?" Becker muttered to himself.

"If it wasn't for that man, we'd all be dead by now," Berlin whispered in his ear, "You'd do well to remember that."

Becker gasped at the way the Corporal spoke to him, but she simply continued on walking. He thought about a response but could see she was built for a fight, far more so than he was.

"I guess Kelly saved your life, too?" he asked Doyle as the former MDF soldier approached.

"More than a few times."

"Yeah, well he might be the best guy in the world, but sometimes he can be a real son of a bitch."

Doyle smiled, and he too carried on past him. Becker sighed and followed them. It took twenty minutes for them to reach the top at their careful pace. They finally lay down at the crest and looked in awe at the lines of Krys aircraft in the distance. Most were just inside the hangars with the doors open and visible, with more on the strips out front.

"Wow, how many they have got down there?"

"Thirty, forty craft," said Kelly, studying them carefully, "Maybe a few more."

"What about troops?" Reynolds asked.

"Probably a few hundred with that number of craft, possibly more," said Berlin.

Kelly smiled, now that the group was getting into it, but it was up to him to come up with the plan.

"We can't go in for any prolonged fight, and we don't any heavy hardware. The way I see it, the most damage we can do is against those craft while they're on the ground. They don't shoot back without crews, but in the air they're killing us. We remove their capacity to rule the skies and cover these areas at such speed, and we give ourselves a whole lot bigger chance of going on."

"Few tanks and we could roll in there without issue. Would be a party," said Becker.

"Too slow, even if we had them."

"So how do we do it, Boss?" asked Becker.

Kelly studied the scene once again and racked his brain.

"You know I once read about something just like this. A way of doing this with a handful of soldiers and a few vehicles."

"In what history book could you have read about this?" Becker asked, cynically, "What to do when aliens conquer the earth?"

"Seriously. The only things we have in our favour are the element of surprise and speed."

"Okay, enlighten us."

"Eight vehicles, rigged up with all the hardware we can put on them. We hit at dusk. Use the last of the light. We go in, one pass down the airstrip blowing the hell out of everything we see there. We don't slow down, and we don't stop. One pass along the line and right back out; we vanish into the night. A few minutes, and it's all over."

"You said you read about this?"

"Yes, Becker."

"And did it work?"

"Damn right it did."

"I like it," Becker finally added, to all their surprise.

It was the only positive thing he had said since they went out there, and Kelly could tell it had come together. "All right then, let's go back. We've got work to do."

The next day went quickly, and Kelly found himself rolling up to the base once again, but this time in daylight hours.

"We should have come up in the night and waited out a day," he said to Becker.

"Then why didn't we?"

"Because time isn't on our side."

He was driving the lead vehicle, and they were just a few hundred metres from the hill they had observed from the night before. He brought the column to a halt and rushed up to the hilltop position. The sun was going down now, and it was a beautiful sight. The last of the sun's rays glinted off of the snow-covered scenery.

Other than the daylight, the scene was just as he remembered it. He rushed back down to his vehicle and jumped in.

"We're good to go."

He rolled the vehicles forward and looked to Becker. He was sitting in front of a mounted machine gun fitted on the cowl. He had his slim line tankers helmet on and seemed surprisingly calm.

"You know it's not so bad once you're past the point of no return," he said with a smile.

"When we get onto that strip, you pull that trigger, and you don't stop until the magazine is dry. You change over quickly and you keep firing. You got that?" Kelly said.

"Got it."

He turned to the other two in the back who were manning weapons mounted on the roll case. The rear of the jeep was packed out with magazines.

"So those history books you learned about this from? Did they survive?"

"Mostly, but then, they didn't have the whole world

against them."

"Good enough."

Kelly put his foot to the floor, and the vehicle soared forwards. They reached the treeline where the mud track expanded out into an open plain that was covered in untouched snow. Kelly's jeep flew out off of the embankment and lifted slightly into the air before landing smoothly on its soft suspension and racing across the plain. The sunlight was almost gone now, with just ten minutes left at most.

They all expected to hear gunfire at any moment, but it never came. They reached the rear of one of the hangars without any resistance at all. Their engines made almost no noise, and that was appreciated as they stormed into the enemy base. They got to the front of the hangar and burst out onto the open landing stip.

Becker was on the trigger as Kelly turned sharply to run the length of the hangars. The first of the Captain's shots went wide, but he didn't release his grip on the trigger. He swivelled the gun around on its mounts and panned until the shots hit the first of the Mech aircraft.

The dark landing strip was lit up with hundreds of rounds of tracer fire pouring out from the lead vehicle alone until the next joined in the action. They were firing from both sides of every vehicle and those mounted over the hoods. The first aircraft burst into flames when its ammo rack was hit, but that was only the signal to open up on the next target.

Explosions lit up the area all along the hangar bays as they rode along at a steady pace. Kelly could see a number of silhouettes in the distance moving to head them off. He pointed for Becker and yelled, "Take them!"

Becker rotated the twin-linked weapon around and kept on firing. The three unarmoured creatures were cut down in seconds by a hail of automatic fire. Kelly looked back to see lines of the Mech aircraft burning and smashed. Becker slammed in two new clips, and they kept up the shooting for another couple of minutes until they reached the end of the line. As they did so, they saw a search light pan onto their position from a tower up ahead. Two pulses struck the ground around them, but Becker and the other gunners quickly returned fire.

The searchlight was blown out after the initial volley, and soon after the tower exploded and was engulfed with flames.

"We got you!" Becker shouted.

He turned his fire to the last of the aircraft on the ground and emptied his magazines on them. Kelly could see a hive of activity back towards the first hangar where they had started at. It brought a smile to his face to see so many Mech aircraft wrecked in their wake, but he knew it was time to get the hell out.

Kelly turned the wheel sharply and led the convoy around the last hangar, putting his foot on the gas once again to race across the snow as fast as they possibly could. A number of pulses rushed past them and hit the trees ahead, causing a few to set alight.

"Almost there, come on!"

Something splashed onto the inside of the windscreen and Kelly looked back. Doyle was sprawled over his machine gun and gasping for air. As they reached the fire of the trees, he could see the blood splattered over his own shoulder and inside of the cockpit.

"Hold on, you're gonna make it!"

They hit the ramp leading to the track far faster than the first time, in the desperation to escape. The jeep launched twice the distance into the air this time and landed hard. The back end veered out of control, and only the forward motion caught it and brought it back in line. They thundered on through the tree-covered lane.

"He's hurt badly!" Berlin called out.

Kelly glanced back and saw the Corporal trying to treat him, but he looked severely wounded. Kelly wanted nothing more than to stop and lend some help, but he knew they couldn't afford to. Kelly wrestled the wheel as they slid through the track at a speed only a maniac would travel, but somehow the rest of the column managed to keep up.

"Wow, we did it!" yelled Becker in excitement.

He looked over to Kelly; surprised to see the Commander wasn't celebrating. He glanced back now and saw Doyle in the Corporal's arms. They went on for more than a kilometre when Kelly finally put on the brakes and brought them to a halt. He got out and went to the back of the vehicle to check on his old friend.

Doyle wasn't moving, and his uniform was soaked in blood. Corporal Berlin had tears dripping down her face, the only time any of them had ever seen such a thing.

"Did he say anything to you?" Kelly asked.

She shook her head. Kelly sighed as he mourned his friend, knowing there was nothing more he could do. The vehicle behind him had taken a pulse across its fender, and the driver was cut and bleeding from shrapnel. He suspected there was plenty more damage he couldn't see, but there was no time to look.

"We have to go, Kelly," said Becker.

But he didn't move for a moment.

"Kelly!"

He snapped out of it and jumped into the driver's seat.

"The price, it never seems worth paying afterwards," he replied.

Becker knew how he felt, but more than anything because of the responsibility he had to endure.

"We've all lost, and it never feels good."

Kelly fired up the engine and pulled off into the night once again. He could feel a tear come to his eye. He turned and wiped it before anyone could notice as he pulled on his night vision glasses and carried on home.

When they finally reached the encampment, they approached slowly and quietly. There were only a couple of hours left to daylight, and several were already awake, or couldn't sleep due to the cold. Kelly brought his vehicle to a halt, and then went to the back with the other two to help lift Doyle's body out.

Kelly looked at the body of his friend as they laid him down, and then over to the other crews who carried another one of their fallen and several wounded.

"Was it worth it?"

Kelly nodded to Becker before responding. "There are casualties in war. They never feel worth it, not even after victory. Let's get them buried. We'll have a service when everyone wakes in a couple of hours."

Kelly dug the grave for Doyle himself, and Becker helped him do it. By the time the sun was coming up, most of the group had gathered around to pay their respects. Kelly hadn't even counted their number recently, but he knew it couldn't be much more than a couple of hundred. Everybody stood silently and waited for him to address them.

"Last night we conducted an operation with the intention of severely hindering enemy actions within this province. We succeeded in that mission, and these two fighters, these two friends were vital in the accomplishment of that mission. They aren't the first casualties of this war, and neither will they be the last. Know that they have found peace now and left this wretched fighting behind."

He stepped forward and took up the body of Doyle, with Becker helping. They lowered him down into the grave and began to replace the soil over his body. It was the best burial they could give him. As they placed the last of the earth over the two bodies, the crowd began to disperse, but Kelly stayed put. Becker was about to say something when they heard the roar of engines overhead and saw dozens of Mech craft soar into view. Kelly didn't even respond as dozens more arrived.

"Kelly! Get down!" Becker hollered.

The Captain rushed over and grabbed Kelly, hauling them both to shelter beside the nearest vehicle. Becker grabbed a rifle and began to fire at one of the craft. Guns mounted on the vehicles roared to life from their people rushing to crew them, but dozens of Mechs were already descending in amongst them.

Kelly got to his feet and grabbed a rifle, but as he took aim realised how hopeless it was. Two of the enemy aircraft were shot out of the sky, and a few more would soon join them, but there were dozens more joining them. He looked around at the pulses landing everywhere, and many of their people being struck by the weapons.

"It's over," he whispered.

Becker was firing in all directions like a mad man and didn't hear him.

"Come on, Kelly, shoot something!"

Pulses continued to rage down upon them, and Kelly saw two of their own launched through the air and land smouldering on the snow. He threw down his rifle and walked out into the open empty handed.

"What are you doing, Kelly!"

"It's over, Becker! Put down your weapons! Stop fighting!"

The shooting continued on for a moment before several others seemed to notice, and the Mechs came to a standstill. Becker got out from cover and looked at the bizarre scene with amazement. There were thirty or forty Mechs amongst them now, and not one of them moved. The gunfire from their own side quickly died down, and many got out from cover to marvel at the sight. Then they looked to Kelly.

"It's over!" he yelled again. "Put down your weapons!"

Becker couldn't believe what he was hearing.

"After all this, we just give up?"

"I don't know what more to say to you," replied Kelly, "I have done everything I can. I have fought all I can and done what I was thought best in every situation, but look!"

He pointed to the Mech craft hovering above them and the Mechs surrounding their people. As he said it, another two-dozen dropped down to the ground and held pulse cannons at the ready, without actually firing.

"If we keep up this fight, then we're already dead. Lay down your weapons, and live to fight another day!"

He could hear his voice quivering, finding it so difficult to say the words, but he knew it was what they had to do.

"Put them down!"

Becker was the first to do so but still muttered under his breath, and the rest soon followed. He dropped his rifle and slumped down onto the front bumper of the vehicle he had been sheltering behind. The rest soon followed and surrendered their weapons.

"Why have they stopped firing? Why don't they just finish us?"

"I don't know, Reynolds, but we were finished if we kept fighting. At least this way we might have a chance."

"Should have gone down fighting like we would have at the Drachenburg," said Becker.

"Then I am sorry I failed you, and I am sorry you followed me," replied Kelly with bitter sorrow in his tone.

* * *

"Colonel Taylor, come with me," stated Irala.

He was pouring water down his throat and all over his face. He was still dripping in sweat from the continuation of their training.

"Just give me a few minutes, will you?"

"No, you will want to see this now."

He sighed and got to his feet.

"You know you make us wait days or weeks on end for

you, and then expect us to snap to attention when it suits you. Do you know how annoying that is?"

"Yes," he replied in an oddly straight fashion.

"Well, good, at least we understand each other."

Irala led him just a few metres away from the group to where there was open space. It was where they had been training until moments before. He then stopped.

Taylor shrugged, as if to ask what they were doing.

"The man you went to Earth to see. Commander Kelly."

"What of him?"

"He and his people were ambushed approximately six hours ago."

Taylor felt his heart sink and was just waiting to hear that Kelly was gone.

"Any survivors?"

Irala said nothing. He simply turned and seemed to operate a few controls on the forearm of his armour. A moment later a large screen projected out before them. It was ten metres wide and in the open for all to see. It was one of the drone feeds. At first the view was drawn back showing much of Northern Europe.

"What is this?"

Taylor looked back to Parker and raised his hand to call silence. They watched the video screen zoom in further and further. But they were not looking at Germany. The camera was heading for France and focused down onto Paris. Finally, it reached that same point at Taylor's statue that he had been shown before.

"What has this got to do with anything?" whispered Taylor.

Then he noticed the shapes of humans. At least a hundred and fifty of them were formed up loosely, with Mech warriors surrounding their prisoners. At the front of the line was Kelly.

"They're alive?" Taylor asked in amazement.

Gasps rang out behind them as the rest of the unit realised what they were seeing.

"Why are they still alive? How?"

He watched the figures of several of the Mech elite stroll out towards them and stop. Finally, Erdogan strode out from a nearby building and stood before Kelly. The creature was unmistakeable even from a bird's eye view. They stood opposite each other as if talking when Erdogan violently lashed out with a punch to Kelly's face. It was enough to cause him to stagger back a few paces before regaining his feet. As he did so, one of the other humans rushed out towards Erdogan as if to assault him. A pulse cannon flashed, and the man dropped dead before Erdogan.

"Why are they keeping them alive?"

As Taylor asked it, they saw cloud cover begin to obscure the scene, and the feed was lost all together. Nobody said a word for almost a full minute as they tried to take it all in. Eventually, it was Silva's growly voice that piped up.

"We're going in to get 'em, right, Sir?"

Taylor turned back to his unit and could see they were all of one mind.

"Damn right we are."

"Erdogan wants you to do this. It is a trap," added Irala.

"Yep, but we know it's a trap, so we'll just have to outsmart him. Better still, we know where he is."

"We did. But by the time we could reach that position, he may well be long gone."

"Worth a shot though, don't you think? That bastard is rubbing this in our faces, and I think we have a chance to humiliate him, and rescue some of our own in the process. Hell, we even have a chance to take him on. That's what we've been aiming for, isn't it?"

"Erdogan would not set a trap for us, and then risk himself in doing so."

"Okay, so we get two out of three things we want. That ain't so bad."

Irala went silent. He seemed to be thinking about the situation, as he often did.

"Are you conferring with your people?" Taylor asked.

"Yes."

It confirmed what he had always wondered.

"This is not the best course of action, but if you are for it, then we will help you."

Kelly couldn't believe they finally had their shot. He was almost overcome with excitement, even though he knew the dangers they were about to face. "Thank you. You don't know how much this will mean to my people."

"If you succeed."

"It's the right thing to do, whether we succeed or not, and they know that."

"I would like to know one thing, Colonel."

"Anything, Irala."

"Were it me and my people down there, would you come for us?"

"Yes," he replied confidently, "Anyone who fights with us would get my help, and if you ever need it, know that I will be coming for you."

"Then we will provide you five of our ships and twenty of our Kaitiaki, the machines that you have seen."

"The what?"

"You may call them Guardians. They will be commanded by my people from the safety of their vessels, and they will default to your command if control by us is lost."

"I don't know how to thank you."

He stepped past the alien and before his own Regiment.

"Training is over! It's time to take the fight to them!"

CHAPTER TWELVE

"Sure feels good to be going home!" Rains exclaimed.

The others were silent as they wondered what they might face. The Mastiff was crammed with fifty of the Inter-Allied marines and three Guardians. They had to crawl in and stay hunched due to their height. Jafar watched them carefully at all times. Taylor couldn't blame him; after all, they had tried to kill him.

"You know how crazy and stupid this is, right?"

"Yeah, Eli, but it makes all the sense in the world, doesn't it?"

"Do you really believe this plan can work, Mitch?"

"Wouldn't be here if I didn't."

"We're jumping in five...four...three," Rains said, counting down.

From the cockpit of the Mastiff, they could see nothing but the hangar bay of the Diderot displayed on the screens around them. They felt a lurch when they were taken into the space gateway. It was always a bizarre feeling, almost like the rush you felt in your stomach when leaping out of an aircraft.

"We're through!"

Rains studied the screens before him and shook his head in amazement. Well, I'll be damned. "Right inside the atmo, just as they said we would be."

The hangar bay doors slid open, and they were met with the most beautiful of sights. It was noon over Paris, and the clear blue skies allowed them to see for as far as their eyes could, but it was still just on their camera feeds. Rains got on the power, and they burst out of the hangar bay and initially dropped like a stone before gaining some altitude.

"She ain't built for smooth flying!"

Pulses flashed around them from the anti-aircraft weapons opening fire. One struck the fuselage, and they rocked violently but continued on without any adverse effect.

"Yep, that's why I love this bird," Rains said quietly to himself.

Taylor was looking at the rear screens as the last of the friendly craft departed from the Diderot. With the Connolly, and their two alien escort vessels, she jumped back out.

"All alone now," said Rains.

"No, they haven't left. They'll be back."

They saw a flash in the sky a few kilometres off as the second part of the fleet arrived and began to launch its assault craft. Pulses filled the sky now as the anti-aircraft defences fired with everything they had. Taylor looked down at his watch and counted the seconds, "Three, two, one.."

They watched on the screens as three nuclear weapons ignited a few kilometres away at a Mech base. Rays of light from the Aranui struck the surface at strategic targets, but the attack lasted less than thirty seconds. They watched the second wave of ships jump back out of the area, and all that was left were the wave of assault craft heading for the centre of Paris.

"Two thousand against a city," said Parker.

"Yeah, Eli, but we just evened up the odds a little."

"Erdogan was never going to be here, was he?"

Taylor shook his head. "Trap or not, he'd be a fool to risk himself in it. He's many things, but not a fool."

"And this trap, how exactly are we not gonna fall into it?" Rains asked.

"Erdogan will have expected a covert strike to get Kelly's people out. He's studied us, and he knows that's what we do. Not an offensive of this nature."

"Probably because to attack the city would be insane."

"We've hit key installations around the city. They'll be in absolute chaos for some time. And Irala has put in jammers to block their communications for a ten kilometre radius."

"He can do that?" Parker asked.

"Yeah, he says so. It's about time the Krys felt what it's like for things to go dark. They've got no communication at all, no video feeds, no surveillance. For the time we're here, this is our town."

"All right, we're going in," Rains announced.

Kelly could see his statue at the far end of the long colonnade that ran up to it. He was still amazed it was intact.

"Put us down, right here."

"You got it."

As Rains replied, a huge pulse blast struck the front of their ship and rocked them violently. Damage markers flashed all around Rains' console, and a fire broke out near the bow. Taylor didn't have to say anything; his people were already dealing with it. Rains banked hard as another pulse glanced the hull.

"We aren't landing here!" They flew off to the north as fast as Rains could put the power down.

"We need to get out now!" Taylor hollered.

Lighter pulses continued to smash into their flank as Rains looked for somewhere to land.

"I can't put you on the ground. We'll be swamped!"

"Find me an LZ, anywhere, just do it!"

He looked over and spotted a flat rooftop of what used to be a hospital. It was only four storeys high.

"On top of that do?"

"Will it take the weight?"

Rains shrugged.

"Fuck it, put us down."

Rains brought them in as quickly as he could to avoid the gunfire, using all the power to slow them down right at the last moment. They hit the rooftop harder than he would have wanted and heard the supports of the roof top creak, but they finally they came to a halt.

"Everyone out!" Taylor ordered.

All of the access ramps dropped down, and the marines rushed out as the Guardians squeezed out into the open. Mitch looked around to see they were two kilometres north of their original landing zone, but there was no time to worry about it, anymore. He turned around to see Rains climb out with a rifle in hand.

"Not this time, Lieutenant. You have a job to do. Protect this bird, and make sure she's ready to fly out when we need her."

He turned to one of the Guardians. "You stay here and protect this ship, and protect our pilot. They're our ticket out of here, you got it?"

The Guardian nodded, and Taylor turned to survey the scene. He could see that Mastiffs and other lighter craft were landing all over, but they were all forced to land far from their target.

"Gonna be a long fight to get to that Palace," said

Parker.

Erdogan's Palace was a vast structure. It seemed they had attempted to mimic some of the 19th century architecture that used to stand in its place before the city was flattened. And yet the shape of the structure was where the similarities ended. It was constructed entirely from what looked like raw iron. It was dull and lacklustre, with only a natural grain. The Palace appeared to have been built as a double scale version of a former Royal residence he remembered seeing in photographs years ago. There was no iconography on the structure at all, not even a flag. It was a stark sight.

"You think he meant for the place to look like a concrete box?" Silva asked.

"Don't know, don't care," said Taylor, focusing his attention entirely on finding a safe way to reach it. He looked down. A dozen Mechs were approaching across an open square below them.

"Shortest path is right through them," he said.

Without another word, Mitch ran to the edge and jumped off the roof. The others quickly followed. As he made his descent, he used his helmet targeter to fire two shots at the nearest creature. The rounds knocked it back and onto one knee, but it got back up as he landed. He took better aim now and opened fire with a well-aimed burst that pierced the creature's armour at the chest.

The rest of the marines dropped in beside him and

opened fire, but before they had got off a few bursts, they saw light flashing, and a volley of white light smashed into the Mechs. It tore eight of them apart with no effort at all. Taylor saw the Guardians were providing fire from the rooftop where they had stayed. He turned back and continued on firing at the last few, and they were quickly overcome. He stood up in amazement to see the effectiveness of their allies' weapons. Two of the Guardians then jumped from the rooftop and landed hard on the ground beside them. The impacts were so great that the ground cracked before their feet.

Taylor could tell the Aranui Guardians had none of the agility the creatures themselves did, but they more than made up for it with sheer strength and power.

"Damn handy in a tight spot these fellows."

Taylor almost smiled at Silva.

"Move on!" he rushed forward over the bodies of the first creatures. He looked around for any other signs of trouble but couldn't seem to find anyone.

"Seems awfully quiet."

Just as Parker said the words, a pulse struck the ground around them, and several others followed it. They saw a Mech heavy fighter heading right for them from the south. The Guardian on the roof of the hospital had already opened fire but was having difficulty tracking its speed as it soared towards them.

"Take cover!"

They scattered, but the two Guardians stood their ground and fired all their weapons head on into the fighter. Holes were ripped through the cockpit and hull, but there was no stopping it. The aircraft began to dip further and head right for them. Pulses and lasers still smashed into it, but they could not stop the mass of the craft. It plunged into one of the Guardians and ignited on impact. The wreckage burst apart and scattered out around them. Taylor was hunkered down behind his shield and felt the impact of a large piece of shrapnel smash into it. It then bounced over the top and carried on across the square.

"Everyone okay?" he shouted, getting to his feet.

There was not much left to look at of the Guardian who had taken the impact, but the other looked ready to go on. It was a loss they could have done without, but Taylor was glad it was a machine and not one of their own that had fallen. He looked up to check on Rains. He was standing at the edge of the rooftop with the Guardian that had stayed with him. The pilot gave him a salute for good luck. Taylor turned and moved on to find their goal.

He didn't recognise any of the buildings around them. Every single one must have been rebuilt in recent years, or constructed by the enemy.

"Last time I was here, pretty much all that was standing was that stupid statue of me," he said to Parker.

"Stupid? So it doesn't piss you off that Erdogan has claimed it and paraded around it for all to see."

"Damn right it pisses me off. Just because I don't like it, doesn't mean I don't want it."

They passed through an opening between two buildings and came out at a large open square. They could see Captain King a hundred metres at one end, doing battle with the enemy.

"Where are all the people?"

"What people, Silva?" Parker asked.

"Humans. Irala said they didn't kill them all."

"Wouldn't want them ruining the look of the city though, would you?" Taylor joked, "When would you ever have a conquered populace still living beside the ruler's palace? I'd say Erdogan intends to rebuild this city into what it once was."

"I'd rather see it flattened again than that."

"Amen, Eli."

They were running at a steady pace across the square, heading towards the narrowing street that would lead to the Palace. Taylor was brought to a standstill and froze when they took the bend into the narrow street. They found a Juggernaut standing guard.

"Oh, shit," whispered Parker.

"Get that pig deployed, now," Taylor said.

But it was too late. The creature had already spotted them. It leapt forward and rushed at them. It was a terrifying sight. They all knew how hard they were to kill, and how much damage they could deal.

"Fire!"

But before they could pull the triggers, the Guardian rushed forward. It fired both its weapons and headed straight for the creature. The impacts blew holes in its armour until finally they clashed. They both stopped both dead as they slammed into one another. The creature tried to take a hold, but the Guardian drove its fist into one of the holes it had shot in the armour. The strike prised the armour open like a tin can, and then it fired its arm-mounted cannon from inside. The Juggernaut went limp, and the Guardian tossed it aside like garbage.

"The day we make suits like that, I want one," said Silva.

Taylor continued on and reached the entrance to the square they had so recently flown over. At the far end was his statue, still untouched by the war. At the entrance to the Palace were a dozen Mechs. They stood on guard as if nothing had happened.

"They're like statues," said Parker.

"More like bowling pins waiting to be knocked down," Silva grinned.

Taylor liked the idea.

"Those aren't Erdogan's guards," said Jafar.

"What's that mean? He ain't home?"

"Yes."

"Ah, well, his home is still our playground. Let's do this."

The open stretch to the Palace was two hundred metres

long, with water running down a several metre-wide stretch in the centre and steel colonnades along the whole length. The group spread out and staggered themselves, beginning their advance at a steady pace. The moment they entered the path leading to Palace, the Mechs sprung into action as if activated through the movement they detected. Taylor upped the pace and targeted the first with his rifle, opening fire as they got to a hundred metres. Rays of light surged out of the Guardian's weapons soon after, and the rest of them joined the fight.

The Palace guards were slightly larger than the normal Mechs, and they all carried shields and glaive like weapons. They pointed the glaives forward, presenting gun barrels at their tips, and opened fire. Their shields largely absorbed the shots of each side's weapons. Only the Guardian's powerful weapons were breaching the shields. Taylor kept up the fire to cover their advance until he was within twenty metres.

He dropped his rifle to his side, drew out his Assegai, and increased the pace to a full on spring. He crashed into the first creature's shield, and its sloped guard caused him to ramp up it and flip over the top of the creature. As he rolled over the top, he descended on the Mech in front; his Assegai driving straight down into its collar, and he collapsed on top of the beast. Jafar impaled the first one he had encountered.

By the time Taylor got to his feet, there were none of

the enemy left standing, and only the last couple were being finished off on the ground.

"Not Erdogan's guards, you say? Just as well, as they aren't up to much."

"Why hasn't he hit us yet with everything he's got?"

"Because, Parker, the Aranui are making diversionary attacks on two other continents, and because of the signal jamming they have set up here. Erdogan has no idea we're even here. And if everything works as it should, he won't till we're out of here."

"You really think that'll play out that way?"

"We've made it this far."

"And you're sure Kelly is in here?"

"Enough questions already," replied Taylor.

He walked up to the vast doors of the entrance to the Palace. They were five metres wide and even more in height. He rested his hand on the doors and pushed, as if expecting them to open.

"Breaching charge," he said quietly.

"Two of the marines stepped forward and slapped charges onto the metalwork. The others took cover.

"Fire in the hole!"

Dust and debris filled the air from the charge exploding. Taylor stepped up to the entrance; they had barely even scratched the surface.

"Shit," said Silva, looking at how little impact the device had.

The Guardian stepped forward, and panels on its right thigh opened and revealed a domed metallic device half a metre wide. They cleared the way as it strode up to the doorway. It pushed the device into position, and it clamped on like a powerful magnet.

"Get back!" Taylor gave the order.

"What are you expecting, Mitch?"

"I have no idea, Eli, but Irala's people don't mess around and do things by half measures!"

They were twenty metres back when the Guardian seemed to activate a switch on a control panel in its arm. A pulsating sound rang out that got louder until it was like a subwoofer next to your ear. Suddenly, the dome erupted into a three metre wide ball of light for just a few seconds and then vanished.

Many of them gasped at what they saw. Everything that was within the ball of light had just disappeared and been cut away. Shards of metal were smouldering and white hot. Even a part of the floor had gone.

"Now that's what I call a breaching charge," said Silva.

"All right, what are you waiting for?" Taylor asked, "Go!"

The first marine through the breach was cut down by a dozen pulses, but Jafar and the Guardian made it through after her. Taylor was in the second rank and could see the entrance was an all out melee. Twenty Mechs were fighting them in hand-to-hand combat. He looked for the nearest target he could find, a Mech already fighting Silva. Taylor ducked down and thrust his Assegai into the creature's leg. The pain forced it to drop its shield slightly, just enough for Silva to thrust over the top and into its face, killing it instantly.

He turned around in time to see the Guardian stamp one to death while shooting another, and throwing yet another across the room. Taylor smashed the edge of his shield into the flank of a Mech, allowing one of his marines to finish it off. Yet another of theirs had fallen, but the Mechs were defeated. Parker was about to drive her Assegai down into the face of one of the wounded Mechs that lay on its knees when Jafar yelled, "Stop!"

She did so, but they were all amazed at what appeared to be empathy and compassion from their friend who had killed so many of his own. He strode up to the Mech. He put his hand around the back of its head and released the clamps of part of its suit until its head became visible to everyone. It was clear the creature was wounded, and blood was trailing from its mouth. Half of them expected Jafar to show some mercy, but instead he raised his Assegai and placed the burning hot tip against the side of its face. It winced in pain.

"Where are the humans?" Jafar asked sternly.

No response came, so he touched the Assegai onto the creature's face again. Smoke rose as its flesh burned again.

"Tell me where the humans are, and this can all be

over."

Despite all the dead lying around them that they had caused, torture brought them all to a standstill. It was a strange sight to behold, even though they hated Jafar's victim. Taylor wanted to tell him to stop, but somehow he couldn't. Jafar raised the creature's arm and thrust the Assegai into it. He put it just far enough to cause immense pain, without killing it. He then drove the blade down into the joint of its kneecap, and finally the creature screamed in pain.

"Where?"

The Mech said something in their own language, and the words appeared scathing and angry even though they meant nothing to Taylor. Jafar made his retort by driving his Assegai down into the creature's collar and killed it.

"You find out?" Taylor asked.

"They are being held in a prison below the surface."

"Under this Palace?"

Jafar nodded.

"Well, then, lead the way."

They got moving. Taylor was beside Jafar as he led the group.

"What did he say to you?"

"He insulted my heritage."

"And do you care about that?"

"When he was alive, yes, but a dead man can cause no offence."

"I'm not so sure about that."

They arrived at a large oval room. One side descended into a broad ramp going beneath the surface, just as Jafar had said. At the base of the ramp, some thirty metres down, was a large shutter door that was sealed with no windows. They reached a control panel, and Parker went to work on trying to jerry rig it. As she did, the Guardian strode up to the shutter and took a hold of the base and ripped it upwards. The shutter flew up and ravelled onto the spool above them. To all their amazement, they had found Kelly and the rest of his people. They were behind one large set of prison bars and then divided into smaller cells. There was no sign of aliens anywhere.

At first they all looked to the Guardian in a terrified fashion, but their attention was soon taken over by Taylor who they all recognised.

"Taylor?" Kelly stammered, "How can you be here?"

"I told you I'd come, old friend. I just didn't think it would have to be so soon."

"I'm sorry. We were doing okay, but we tried to punch over our weight."

"They say you knocked out a hundred enemy aircraft, and that's why you're here?"

"A hundred might be exaggerating a tad, but I'll run with it."

Kelly looked around to see he recognised many of the faces, and amongst them was Becker staring back at him.

"How you made it is a mystery," stated Taylor.

"Yeah, thanks. You here to rescue us or talk us to death?"

Taylor looked to Jafar and the Guardian and pointed to the two gates at the centre of the bars. They took hold of one each and wrenched them apart.

"What is that?" Kelly asked.

"It's a long story is what it is, for when we're long gone from here."

"So you aren't here to stay and help us fight?"

Taylor could see in his eyes that it was what he had been hoping for.

"We'll be back for Earth, but right now, we just need to go on living and get ready for our home coming. Are your weapons and armour here?"

"Locked in a vault behind these cells."

"Jafar, get that door open, and take...the Guardian with you."

The Aranui Guardian seemed so alive it felt as if it should have a name. Taylor drew out his Assegai and drove it through the lock on the cell Kelly shared with five others. He pulled open the door. Kelly rushed forward and wrapped his arms around the Colonel in a bear hug.

"Damn good to see you, Colonel."

"You saw me a couple of days ago."

Kelly looked at him blankly.

"When I was projected down to your camp."

"Ahhh...yes...but...that wasn't really you."

He was ecstatic and smiling like a lunatic.

It wasn't long before Kelly's people were set free, and they were running to the vault to grab their gear. Kelly reappeared before them in a Reitech suit that was barely recognisable. His uniform looked a murky grey and brown, and his suit was heavily weathered. He carried a shield with a fist-size hole in the top left corner and wore no helmet at all. Most of the others looked similar, and Becker was covered in dirt and grime.

"Are your people up to this?"

"Always, Colonel. Can you get us out?"

"Wouldn't have come if I couldn't."

CHAPTER THIRTEEN

Kelly peered out of the hole they had blown in the Palace entrance. He half expected to see an army waiting to oppose then, but to his surprise there was nothing more insight than the bodies they had left outside. He looked back to the group.

"It's clear!" he smiled.

He turned back and the grin was soon lost when he saw Mechs drop into view. First it was just a handful, and then they began dropping in between the colonnades by their dozens.

"No it ain't!" he added.

Silva stepped up to him to see what they faced.

"Knew it couldn't be that easy."

Taylor agreed, "I'd be worried if it was."

He looked back to the group who were waiting to move. Almost fifty of his own and three times that number of

Kelly's people.

"Few hundred of them against a few hundred of us, I give us the odds. They're all that stands in the way of the completion of this mission. There is no going around. There is no plan B."

With that, he stepped out of the hole and into the daylight. None of the Mechs fired upon him. He moved calmly and casually to the edge of the steps leading up to the Palace. His comrades and allies poured out of the doorway to take up position at his side and back. The Mechs slightly outnumbered them. Taylor had no doubt they could win, but it would be a costly battle.

The two sides simply stared at each other, waiting for the other side to make a move. Then out of nowhere, a volley of white pulses smashed into the Mechs in front of them. The marines watched in amazement as beams followed them and tore the creatures apart as they scattered. Taylor looked up. One of the Aranui vessels in the sky was raining down fire on their foes.

"Let's mop up!" he yelled.

He raised his rifle, took aim, and joined the fight. The enemy were dropping like flies, and he watched the joy on Kelly's face as he joined in the slaughtering. The Aranui vessel finished up and moved out. Three quarters of the Mechs were dead or dying now. Some were firing back, but they were already being picked off by many of his side.

"Forward!"

He rushed at the head of the line and opened fire with his rifle. He struck two of the Mechs when his magazine went dry, but he had no time to stop. He drew out his Assegai and carried on at a jogging pace. He approached the first creature that came at him with its shield held out and extended. Taylor struck the shield on the right-hand side. It pivoted in its hands, revealing an opening to the neck. Taylor quickly jumped and thrust into its exposed neck. He bounced off the side of the beast and spun, regained his feet, and kept running.

The Mech dropped dead behind him, but he didn't even turn to check. He upped his pace towards the street where they had encountered the Juggernaut. Pulses and rays of light smashed their position ahead as the Guardian weighed in on the fight.

He reached the narrow corridor quickly and found just a handful of Mechs advancing through it. With his turn of speed, he was still leading the way, but Jafar was not far behind. Taylor felt the impact of two pulses splash over his shield. He tilted it back slightly and hit the first Mech in the legs. It collapsed onto the top of it, and he pushed the beast off so that it fell face first to the ground. He left it for Jafar to thrust it in the back as he went past.

Taylor rushed at the next and ducked under a strike from a glaive, turning to strike back when he felt an impact across his back. It hit so hard, he felt himself fall to his knees from the force of the blast. Jafar rushed past him and charged at the creature who had struck him, and Silva was on the other Mech in a split second. Mitch could feel the wind had been taken out of him, and the pain in his shoulders was so immense it hurt as he tried to right his back and stand up. His knees had buckled from the impact, and it was hard to get moving again.

"Mitch, are you okay?" Parker shouted.

He nodded, but he didn't feel okay at all. He put his arm over her shoulders and allowed her to support him as they carried on forwards. Silva took his other arm and helped Mitch along. He couldn't feel any major damage, but his body was weak, and his legs felt even worse. He felt his feet dragging across the floor. Finally, he looked up to see the hospital ahead, and he knew they weren't far now. He watched as Kelly's people were ushered aboard two transports, and then they carried on for the rooftop.

"I got it. I got it," Taylor mumbled.

He gathered his feet, took a few steps to get his bearings, and then started up the stairwell. He was getting feeling back now, but it hurt like hell, but he would be damned if he would be carried out. He fought the pain in his body to reach the top and was met by the welcome face of Rains. The Guardian stood beside him had scorch marks on its body, and one of its arms looked limp.

"Seen a little action?" Taylor asked the Lieutenant.

"Not as much as you, by the looks."

"You ready to get the hell out of here?"

Rains nodded.

"I never thought I'd say it, but get us the hell off this planet."

He staggered on to the inside of the Mastiff and heard the roof creak once again as they began to board.

"Might want to get us moving, Rains, not sure this is gonna support us a whole lot longer!"

Rains watched the last of them board the ship and quickly hit the door switch and fired up the engines. As they burnt into the surface of the roof, they could feel it giving way. They dropped a couple of metres onto the next level as Rains put full power to the engines, and they began to move forward. As they did so, they felt the floor start to give way again. The bow of the ship smashed through interior walls, and finally they burst out into the open air.

"Not the smoothest take off in the world, Lieutenant."

"Smooth is boring, overrated," replied Rains, as he wrestled for control of the Mastiff.

"This thing's like a brick, you know."

"Yeah, and we'd probably not have made it in anything else."

They soared towards the Diderot and landed as hard as they had taken off. As they looked on the rear viewscreens, they could see whole fighter wings on an attack vector. Just as they thought they were stuck there, they soared forwards into a jump gateway. A moment later all they could see on the screen was the blackness of space.

'We made it," said Taylor in amazement.

"We never doubted you," Parker smiled and threw her arm around him.

"Taylor, Taylor, Taylor!" the rest of them aboard the Mastiff began to yell.

"Why?" he asked Parker.

"Because this was your idea. You set out to save our own people, and you succeeded."

"We succeeded."

"But without you, it would never have happened."

"And without all of you, I would never have pulled it off."

The ramps of the Mastiff lowered, and Taylor staggered out to find Kelly and Becker already waiting for them on the landing deck. Taylor shook his head in disbelief as his marines rushed out to mingle with them and talk to old friends.

"How did you pull this off?" Becker asked.

"With the help of the most surprising and amazing people I have ever met. We found another race out here. Wherever the hell here is. They are technologically advanced, and they hate the Krys."

"But how?" Kelly joined in.

"How what?"

"How could you find such a people?"

"Jafar led us here. Quite by accident, by all accounts."

"And they're going to help you re-take Earth?"

"Yeah, can you believe it? Seemingly no hope left at all, and look where we landed. In the hands of another race who despise the Krys just as much as we do."

"What did you have to promise them to get their help?"

"Just a place on Earth. Same thing we're all fighting for."

"And they went for that?"

Taylor sighed. "After a little persuasion, Kelly."

"Well, you are good at that, aren't you?"

Taylor went over to a crate and sat down to rest his feet. He couldn't deal with the questions and the excitement anymore. His legs didn't want hold his body up any longer, and only Parker came to sit with him.

"That's a real kick in the teeth to Erdogan, isn't it?" We got our people out with only a handful of casualties. He's got to be kicking himself."

That got Taylor thinking.

"It was too easy, wasn't it?"

"What do you mean? We worked for that, Mitch."

"We did, but not hard enough. We fled Earth because we were getting our asses kicked. Okay, so we had a little help, but do you really reckon Erdogan would let us shit all over him like that?"

Parker didn't have an answer. She knew deep down that it was a fair concern, so Taylor carried on instead and played Devil's advocate to his own argument.

"Maybe we are that good? Maybe the Aranui made all the difference? Maybe we caught Erdogan with his pants down, but none of that seems all that likely."

"So what are the alternatives? That he wanted us to pull this off? But why?"

Taylor shook his head. He couldn't think of a good reason why, but it still bothered him.

"I'd say we pulled it off because we had a plan, and we executed it right," added Parker.

Kelly walked over to them.

"So what now?"

"On to our temporary home. There are a lot of people waiting to meet you," replied Taylor. He struggled to his feet.

"Oh, and when we reach the surface, I'll need one of you to report immediately to Major Bryan Weller."

Kelly looked confused. "Never heard of him."

"He can be a son of a bitch, but he's a thorough son of a bitch. He'll start the debriefing. We've been away from Earth for some time now. We need a thorough picture of everything you have done and seen. Maybe there'll be nothing of use, but there might be something. Just have someone useful report to him immediately upon our arrival. Time is something we cannot afford to waste."

"Where is he?"

"You'll find him aboard the Hornet. It's been made a medical ship, and he operates research and investigation out of it."

"I'll send Captain Reynolds. He'll be more than capable."

Taylor nodded in appreciation.

Rains finally stepped up to join them and slapped his hand down on Kelly's shoulder.

"See, we got your ass out."

"And much appreciated it is. That was some fine flying."

Rains laughed. "No, that was some god awful stupid flying, but we survived, so who can complain?

Taylor backed off and sat down again to rest. He felt his back creak, and he had immense pain in his left shoulder blade. He unclipped his rifle and laid it down beside him. Parker sat beside him again.

"I never thought we'd see them again," she said.

"No, it's quite remarkable, but there are plenty more groups still fighting on Earth. We need to either support them or get them out in the coming weeks."

The Diderot came in to land on the surface once again, and Taylor sighed in relief that it was all finally over. He felt as if he could rest for a week, and he bet Kelly's people could too. The ramp at the loading bay dropped down to the surface, and the warm air flooded in. They could hear people cheering and clapping outside. Taylor looked to Kelly.

"Send Captain Reynolds to the Major. He can join the festivities later."

Kelly spoke a few words to the Captain. He strode off down the ramp and through the crowds.

"Ready for this?" Taylor asked Kelly.

He couldn't find the words for the occasion.

"We'll have to get you a new uniform by tomorrow. Can't have you in those rags, anymore."

"I was growing rather fond of them."

They walked towards the edge of the landing bay and looked out to the crowds that had gathered to welcome them to the surface. Irala was the only Aranui among them and stepped up beside Taylor. Kelly looked at him with suspicion.

"Taylor, I must attend to my people. Congratulations."

That was all he said as the hologram vanished.

"He a friend of yours?" Kelly asked.

"I am not sure if I'll ever call him that, but he's certainly an ally, and we wouldn't have gotten your asses home safely without his help."

"I must thank him later."

They carried on down the ramp and were swamped by the crowds.

"Come on, the Admiral will want to meet you!"

The crowds dispersed a little to allow them through but followed on to the landing bay next to the HQ building. The bay was empty, and they were awaiting the arrival of Huang's shuttle.

"Admiral Huber?"

"Huber went down with his ship, Kelly."

"So a lot has changed?"

"And a lot has stayed the same. We still fight to get back to Earth."

They could hear the engines in the sky, and the shuttle soared into view.

"Huang won't want to talk for long. Then we'll find you some food and more than a few beers."

"Sounds good."

He sounded distracted as he watched the descent of the shuttle before them. It finally put down, and they all waited in silence for the ramp to lower and the Admiral to step out to greet them. He came out in full dress uniform that sported more medals and braid than Taylor could imagine. It brought a smirk to Taylor's face, but he refrained from laughing.

Six of his personal command staff and two of his marines accompanied Huang. Taylor didn't call anyone to attention or even bother to salute. They were too caught up in the moment of celebrating their victory.

"Congratulations and welcome!" Huang shouted and strode forward with his arm outstretched towards Kelly.

* * *

Captain Reynolds finally found the Hornet. It was an older model frigate. Crosses had been painted on the side to identify it as a hospital ship, and yet many of the gun turrets and missile platforms remained. He stepped aboard to find it was quiet and calm, not like the rush he would have expected after a battle.

"I'm looking for Major Bryan Weller," he asked a passing nurse.

"Follow this corridor as far as it will go, and you'll find him at the very last door on the left. But, Captain, you'll have to get cleaned up. You can't be in here like that. And you can stow your rifle and other weapons at the armoury."

Reynolds carried on without any concern for the nurse's words. He passed many rooms where he could see personnel resting and recovering from injuries that would soon have them back on duty. He reached the end of the corridor and found a door marked up with Weller's name. He pressed the buzzer and had to wait a few seconds for the door to slide open. The Major sat at a desk at the far end of the small office.

"Captain Reynolds, formerly of the MDF reporting."

"One of Commander Kelly's?"

"Yes, Sir."

Weller smiled. "Then you must be relieved to be back among the fleet. Come on in."

Reynolds took a step into the office. As he passed through the doorframe, it immediately went red and a siren began. Weller froze, knowing what he was looking at.

"A clone," he whispered to himself.

Reynolds realised he had been discovered and reached for the rifle slung at his side. Weller too went for the pistol on his belt, and both men pulled the triggers at the same time. Weller took a hit through the left shoulder, but he kept firing repeatedly until the clone of Reynolds was hit six times and launched back out into the corridor. He looked at the body in horror for just a second and then to his wound. He had no feeling in his left arm at all, and he didn't know much longer he could stay conscious. He laid the pistol down on the desk and hit the comms channel button.

"Put me through to Colonel Taylor, now!" he screamed.

A moment later the sound of chatter and cheering came over the comms channel and Taylor asking, "What is it? I'm a little busy."

"They're clones, clones!" he shouted back with all the strength he could muster.

Taylor looked back to Kelly in horror and could see he had heard the warning, too. Something seemed to click in Kelly's eyes, and he became an entirely different person. He raised his rifle and fired a burst into Huang's chest. The shots went right through the Admiral and struck one of his officers behind. A second later, gunfire erupted as the rest of the clones opened fire on the command staff and the crowd.

Taylor reached for his pistol, but the Becker clone already had him in sight. As Becker pulled the trigger,

Parker leapt in front of Taylor and fired with her pistol. One of the shots skimmed Becker's left ear, but five of his shots struck Parker. Three glanced off her armour. But one went through her arm and the other her neck. She dropped lifelessly to the ground. Taylor immediately fired a single shot into Becker's head, and he was killed instantly.

Without any concern for what was going on around him, Taylor dropped down to Parker's side. He turned her over and could see she was fighting to breathe. He tried to say something to her but couldn't find the words. A few seconds later, she stopped breathing, and her blood poured out over the sand and onto Taylor's hands. For a moment, he was frozen in horror at what he had seen, but it was soon replaced by bitterness and anger. He switched his pistol to his left hand and drew out his Assegai before standing up to join the fight.

Bodies lay scattered all around as both sides opened up with automatic weapons, and nobody carried shields. It was butchery on both sides as there was so little cover to be had. A dozen of the Inter-Allied lay dead around him and dozens more of the crowds that had gathered. Jafar was weighing in against the clones and striking them with a bare hand and his own Assegai as he moved from one to another.

Shots flew all around Taylor, but he didn't care. He stood tall and looked for Kelly's clone. As soon as he identified him, he strode right for him with raw determination and hatred. One of the clones stood in his way and tried to fire, but he spun out and past the barrel, and drove his assegai into their flank before firing a shot into the back of its head.

Finally, he had a clear view of Kelly and sprinted towards him. The Commander's clone noticed his charge and got two shots off. One glanced off his breastplate; the other struck the edge of his arm and opened up a small wound. He dropped the pistol, but it wasn't enough to stop him.

Taylor got past the barrel of the gun and punched the clone in the face with the fist that clenched his Assegai. As he did so, he ripped the rifle out of Kelly's arms and threw it to the ground. The clone drew out its Assegai and readied itself. It felt utterly bizarre to square off against what looked like a close friend, but he wasn't going to let that get in the way of what had to be done.

Kelly's clone lunged forward, and Taylor dodged it. He grabbed hold of his weapon arm at the wrist and drove his Assegai into the gap in the armour by the armpit. The clone straightened up as the pain surged through its body before Taylor finally drove it home and up to the hilt. The thrust went right through the chest and pierced the heart. Kelly's body went limp, and Taylor let go his grip as it dropped to the floor before him.

He looked down at the red blood that dripped from his Assegai, and it made him feel sick. He knew it was just a clone, but the sight of human blood spilled at his own hands was revolting to him after so many years of fighting the Krys.

He thought killing the clone would bring some satisfaction, but it brought none. He just felt empty now. He knew that defeating the clone meant nothing at all.

Screams of pain filled the air, and Taylor turned to look at the damage. The battle had lasted just a few short minutes, and their weapons caused horrific devastation. The clones lay dead or dying, with just a handful detained. He watched Silva put his rifle to the head of one of the prisoners and pull the trigger before moving to the next. Taylor made no attempt to stop him. Hundreds of bodies lay before him. Huang and all of his staff were dead.

Jafar was limping where he had been shot multiple times but still stepped up beside him.

"How did we not see it?" Taylor cried out.

Irala suddenly appeared beside him and looked in horror at what lay before them.

"Where the hell were you?"

"The signal jammer that we sent to protect you in Paris."

"What of it?"

"It was returned to your vessel, the Diderot. We had no idea what was going on until it was too late."

"So he knew," Taylor muttered.

Irala looked confused.

"Erdogan," Taylor said with a growly bitter voice, "He knew what would happen. He knew your tactics, and he used it all against us. Not only have we not succeeded in rescuing our own people, we've just lost more, more than we can afford," he said, looking down at his Eli who lay among the hundreds of dead.

Captain Lasure rushed into view with several of his crew armed and ready for a fight. He stopped at the sight of the bloody scene.

"What? What happened here?"

"Clones. They set a trap, and we played right into it."

Lasure looked over to the body of Huang and gasped again.

"What do we do now?"

Taylor shrugged, unable to speak.

"Bury the dead and keep moving forward!" Silva shouted as he approached.

Taylor nodded in appreciation for the Sergeant Major's help. He always was the man to rely on in the Regiment. Captain Morris was with him. He appeared to be covered in as much of his own blood as others. He couldn't speak a single word as he was still in shock.

"The Admiral is dead. We need to appoint a head of the fleet, even a temporary one, or there will be chaos."

"Then it's you," said Taylor quietly.

"I…I can't. There are many more men and women more suited and better qualified."

"More than anything right now, we need people we can rely on. I am declaring you the head of the fleet, and giving you a field commission to Admiral."

"You cannot do that, Colonel. You know you can't."

"Can't?" he asked, "Anyone who has a problem with this decision can come to me. You are the Admiral now. I hope you live longer than your predecessor," he said bitterly.

Lasure couldn't believe the turn of events, and it was clear he didn't want it, but he had no choice.

* * *

Two days later.

Taylor stood before the graves of all those they were burying, and two thousand or more personnel and civilians stood before him, waiting for him to make some address. He wore a fresh uniform now and had his left arm cradled in a brace. He stood on top of a podium that had been hastily put together from Navy scaffolding. He looked at the lines of graves and openly wept. Irala and fifteen of his own kind were amongst the crowd. It was the most of his people any of them had ever seen in one place, and went a long way to showing respect for their allies.

Taylor looked out to his own Regiment who were present. Many were missing, buried instead of out there where they should be. Large numbers of the crowd were wounded, and many more couldn't make it out of their hospital beds.

Most of all, he thought about Eli Parker. Just one life out of many, but he couldn't help but think of her.

I never believed I would have to bury Eli. I always assumed she would outlive me. Fuck, we were the Immortals!

Despite all the losses they had endured, he could see on the faces of those before him that these were the ones that hit the hardest. They hit when they least expected.

Admiral Lasure stepped up to onto the podium beside him to begin, as he could see Taylor was struggling.

"What you all suffered here was a great loss on both an individual level, and to the fleet at large. Let us ensure that this never happens again. I didn't want this responsibility of being Admiral. You never wanted to lose your friends, and or to be driven from our world. But none of these things can be undone now. We can only look forward."

He looked to Taylor who nodded in appreciation for his efforts. Taylor wiped the tears from his eyes and finally the words came out.

"We lost dearly, friends, comrades, partners, and allies; losses that cannot be replaced with numbers alone, and losses that will never be forgotten. We set out in this war to kill Erdogan and bring an end to it all. But we got distracted. We let our feelings overcome us. I let my feelings lead me. This is a bitter reminder that we lost our way. But now we know it; kill Erdogan. End him in any way we can.

This is all that matters. It doesn't matter how long it takes, how many ships and lives it costs us. Our dead will be honoured with his death. Mourn our dead, and then cast off those feelings and turn them towards him. Erdogan.

Today we mourn. Tomorrow we hunt him down!"